TWEEN FICTION H (NEW)

Dear Anjali

Melissa Glenn Haber

ALADDIN

New York   London   Toronto   Sydney

ALADDIN

An imprint of Simon & Schuster Children's Publishing Division

1230 Avenue of the Americas, New York, NY 10020

First Aladdin hardcover edition July 2010

Copyright © 2010 by Melissa Glenn Haber

For information about special discounts for bulk purchases, please contact Simon & Schuster Special Sales at 1-866-506-1949 or business@simonandschuster.com.

The Simon & Schuster Speakers Bureau can bring authors to your live event. For more information or to book an event contact the Simon & Schuster Speakers Bureau at 1-866-248-3049 or visit our website at www.simonspeakers.com.

Designed by Jessica Handelman

The text of this book was set in Typeka.

Manufactured in the United States of America 0510 MTN

2 4 6 8 10 9 7 5 3 1

Library of Congress Cataloging-in-Publication Data

Haber, Melissa Glenn, 1969-

Dear Anjali / Melissa Glenn Haber. — 1st Aladdin hardcover ed. p. cm.

Summary: When her best friend dies at the age of thirteen, Meredith writes letters to her as she tries to endure her grief and other confusing emotions.

ISBN 978-1-4169-9599-9 (hardcover) ISBN 978-1-4169-9601-9 (eBook)

[1. Grief—Fiction. 2. Best friends—Fiction. 3. Friendship—Fiction. 4. Letters—Fiction.] I. Title.

PZ7.H1142De 2010 [Fic]--dc22 2009032117

In Memoriam

MARTY S. KLEIN

1932–2009

Thanks for the anecdotes.

We miss you.

Sunday, November 15

Dear Anjali,

I really hate it that you're dead.

— I hate it!!!

!!! and !!!!!

That's why I'm writing this on my dad;s old typerwriter

I really have to bludgeon my fingers to pound out the letters and that seems right because it **DOES** hurt and it **SHOULD** hurt to have to write the words that y!o!u!"!r!e! d!e!a!d!

If the universe was the way it should be I would not even be able to write those words

the letters would refuse to print on the page they would **REBEL** because it just does not make sense it is senseless **NONSENSE** that my best friend is suddenly and totally **DEAD!!!!!**

It's so outrageous that I've been thinking I must've heard my mother wrong when she told me except I kind've think I must've heard her right as I just spent the afternoon at your **FUNERAL**

I am still very furious about it actually which is wierd because that is the first Feeling I have had since my mother came into my room and told me the news.

mostly I've been feeling all wierd and numb, like your cheek feels after you've been mauled at the dentist

I've felt so mauled and numb all week so numb I could barely get up this morning and find something black to wear and as a result we were late for your funeral which turned out to be a problem as there were no seats left by the time we arrived

it was so very extraordinarily crowded there that my family had to stand up in the back with all the other indignitaries that got there too late to claim a seat but I got to sit up front with your family because Chandra had saved me a seat there. It was very nice of her but in a way it made me feel even more alone as I've never been with your family without you before and so in the middle of all that damp and weeping crowd I felt most exquisitely and totally alone

it was horrible to feel so alone in the middle of that crowdedness. And it really was really amazingly crowded there so crowded that no one could shut up about it it was like they were all worrying they wouldn't get so many people to show up at their funerals when they died. Later I heard my father saying there are 2 ways to get alot of people at your funeral 1) do alot of things with your life or 2) die before you have a chance to. He sounded kind of bitter when he said it. I guess he's upset because it's too late for him to do either one.

your funeral was apparantly a rousing success on account of it's crowdedness. Everyone was there. Everyone but you, I mean, because it turned out that the actual Anjali Sen was not invited. Instead all the many speakers kept talking about all the things you would;ve done if you'd only lived a long life like a normal person. They kept on saying you would've cured cancer or solved the global warming or averted nucular war and so on but not one of them talked about who you actually **WERE**

that made me very mad because I was in point of fact missing YOU and not the YOU there might've been in the future and that's when I leaned over and told your father I wanted to say something though I had previously resisted--as you know I am not all about the public speaking

As soon as I got up to the podium I instantly regretted it because at that very moment the door opened up and my god you know who came in it was NOAH SPIVAK and I tell you Anjali then I totally wanted to barf and not only because Noah Spivak always makes me want to vomit but also because of the embarasing memory of hanging up on him last Sunday after my mother broke the news to me

I'm not really sure why I called him after all those years of being too shy to say 2 words to him it;s just that I was feeling so **ALONE** after my mother left the room that I started feeling I would float out into black space and never come back if I didn't talk to someone

I was kind of grasping and groping and thinking of you and all those times we talked about Noah Spivak and I kept on remembering that day you said maybe you liked him too and what did I think of that and I don't know it wasn't a good reason or anything but I called him and blurted out the news that you were dead.

There was this sound on the other end of the phone like someone was choking a fish with alot of punctuation marks, like this:

"What???!??!?!???!????!??!???!??!????!!!"

and then suddenly I knew I must've been wrong about what my mother said. Because come on! It doesn't make SENSE to think that someone could be 13 years old one day and the next suddenly and entirely dead It was just impossible and I started feeling very embarased that I had actually for a moment thought that my mother could've possibly said that you had DIED and then the hand holding the phone started to feel all funny and buzzy and then all of me was feeling so buzzy and funny that I could barely hear Noah Spivak over the sound of the voice in my head chanting stupid stupid stupid stupid stupod stupid stupid stupid stuid stupid stupid sfupid stupid stupid stupid stupid stupid stupid stulid stupid stupid tupid stupid stupid stupid stupid stpuid stupid stupid tsupid stupid stupid stupid stupid stupid stupid stupid stupid stupid stupid stoooooooopid and then the voice got so loud and the buzziness so buzzy that I had to hang up. After that I sat on my bed for a long time trying to get up the courage to ask my mother if it was true but I couldn't ask her because I didn't want to have to admit I had thought for a moment that she had said you were dead. Noah Spivak called me back pretty soon after but I didn't answer the phone even though I've been wishing for like 2 years that he would call me. I just let the phone ring and ring and my parents let it ring too. None of us really wanted to talk.

But I guess it turns out I really did hear my mother right because there I was standing up at your funeral about to talk and there was Noah Spivak coming through the door. I watched him try and find a seat in the middle of all that seatless-ness and only belatedly I realized everyone was waiting for me to speak

that was a terrible moment too because I really didn;t know what I wanted to say. I mean I knew I wanted them to know what you meant to me but I didn't know how to say it, how to explain that you were my best friend from the first moment I saw you when we were 4 and how you were going to be my best friend when I was 40 and how you WILL be my best friend FO**REVER** even if you didn't stop the global warming because what mattered to me was not WHAT YOU DID but WHO YOU WERE and WHO

YOU WERE was MY **BEST FRIEND FOREVER**

that's what I wanted them to know but as I was standing up there I knew I just couldn't explain it

I just stood there blabbering and blathering about the last day we spent together, just the Thursday before last, before you got sick. You weren't at all sick then--we never would've thought you were about to get sick. It was just a normal day. We sat in your kitchen like usual and we drank milk like usual and we played Spit like usual, and then I went home. That's what I told everyone. I went home and dropped my stuff next to the radiator in the kitchen like I always do, and my mother looked up from her homework and asked me if I'd had a good time. Of course I had a good time, I told her. I always have a good time with Anjali.

When I was done telling my story I looked out at everyone watching and I could tell my words had not at all conveyed what that day meant to me

everyone was politely waiting for me to get to the POINT of my talking but here's the thing, Anjali:

there wasn't more of a point to it than that. You and me DIDN'T do anything really important that day. Why would we? We didn't know we had to.

"We didn't know it was going to be the last day," I tried. And then it was over, my chance to say how important you were to me. After that some-one else got up and talked about what an amazing world we'd all live in if you'd only been granted another 8 decades or so to invent a Perpetual Motion Glixanator but all I could think about was how you'd never knock over another glass of milk while we were playing Spit at the kitchen table again.

That's what I ended up telling the reporter when she cornered me at the reception.

"You're Meredith Beals, aren't you?" she asked in this bright and fakey voice. "I'm told your just the right person to tell me all about Anjali. I hear she was a VERY SPECIAL little girl."

I kept waiting for you to whack her upside the head from the beyond. Did you know you were a

LITTLE GIRL, Anjali? I was under the impression that you were **THIRTEEN.**

"So tell me, what did Anjali like to do?" the reporter prompted. "What was she good at?"

I tell you, Anjali, that reporter should count herself lucky that i am both a pacifist and a bit of a wimp because otherwise I would have clocked her one myself. Who cares what you were GOOD AT? That's not WHO you were. I mean Wendy Mathinson for example is good at lots of things but that does not mean she is not primarily a class A Acme Brand flying evil BLEEP [that BLEEP is a product of the censoring system my mother installed on my typewriter.] But I couldn't really explain this very well so I told the reporter she should go over and talk to the teachers so they could all tell her what **A SPECIAL LITTLE GRIL** you were who was good at math and who never gave any trouble in the lunch line except maybe that time you kicked Wendy Mathinson on my behalf. Maybe that's what they could put on your tombstone:

ANJALI SEN

SHE WAS GOOD AT MATH

AND NEVER GOT IN TROUBLE IN

THE LUNCH LINE

EXCEPT FOR THAT ONE TIME IN 5TH GRADE

AND THERE WERE EXTENUATING

CIRCUMSTANCES

BECAUSE WENDY MATHINSON IS A BLEEEEEEP

[That bleep is courtesy of the tombstone censoring service]

but really that's not the point Anjali what the
point is is that she was driving me CrAzY what
with point-missing that the stuff that goes on a
tombstone isn't the stuff that matters at all.

It's the little things that mattered to me, not
the big ones

or maybe the little things ARE the big things
in the end, I don't know. But I do k now this: that
reporter was much too dumb to comprehend.

"What about one little detail/" she wheedled

at me. "Don't you want people to know SOMETHING about Anjali? Some little something?"

"FINE," I told her. "You can say Anjali really liked drinking milk." It's true. I KNOW it's true, because I haven't been able to drink milk at all since you died--it's like I have the milk rabies or something. But that reporter didn't even write it down.

"How about this," she said, in one of those teeth-clenched patient voices that tells you the person really wants to smack you. "How about giving me some adjectives? You know, some DESCRIBING words?"

OH SO **THAT"S WHAT A ADJECTIVE IS!!!!** I've been wondering when someone was going to clue me in to that

"Just one teensy little adjective?" she pressed.

Here's the thing, Anjali: I couldn;t, and this is why: as far as I'm concerned there's no DESCRIBING WORD in the whole **ENGLISH LANGUAGE** to describe you, because they've all been used to describe somebody else and that makes them used-up and wrong. The only words that describe you for me are **ANJAL**I and MINE. But I don't think anyone else will ever know what that means.

"Milk-loving," I said at last. "Anjali was a very milk-loving little girl."

The reporter was getting exaggerated.

"Come on, Meredith!" she said. "Don't you want people to know what Anjali was like, now that she's gone?"

"That's the thing of it," I told her heavily, and I meant it. "They CAN'T know what Anjali was like, now that she's gone. You just had to be there."

But then my eyes and my nose were all burn-y so I had to say something to stop myself from crying in front of her. "Fine, listen, you can tell people Anjali really liked to play Spit. That's a card game and we used to play it with these plastic-covered cards with the words to "O Canada" on the back and Anjali was really good at it and once she smacked a card down so hard part of it snapped off. It was the king of clubs and we called it the Stinky King."

But thinking about the Stinky King made me choke up. I don;t even have that any more to remember you by--I gave it to your mother to put in your grave. It was a stupid gesture and a meaningless one because even though I really wanted you to have it with you, now it's gone too and that made me so depressed I told my parents we had to go home. But you probably know that, don't you? Because you must've been there, right? I mean I guess I know you're dead and all but that can't mean you're entirely GONE, can it? How can you be, when I still feel you near me? You CAN'T, that's how--and that's why I'm writing you now and why I promise I will write you EVERY DAY so that you will know how much I miss you and how much I need you and how much I really really hate it that you're dead.

Your best friend,
Meredith

Now I'm back in school but it wasn't my idea. I was planning to continue staring at the cieling for the rest of my life but this morning my mother came in and with limited sympathy announced that I needed to combine my ciriculum of sorrow with a little book learning. So here I am again, but it's not so good. Apparantly Dickson rearranged the desks the day after everyone heard you were dead, e.g. last Tuesday or Wednesday when I was still staring at the cieling. I guess it's smart. It keeps everyone from looking over to the corner and seeing your empty desk and thinking <u>Anjali Sen is dead dead dead dead dead</u>. Now instead they can pretend you never existed at all. That is probably easier for everyone else to handle but it is not easier for me.

It is just so WIERD that your desk is gone! I wonder

what they did with all the stuff that was in it? I bet next time someone gets your books someone else is going to say OOOO you have the book from the girl who died just like I did that time Colette Soulier got the book Kristi Lawrence had before she drownded. But what about the notes and stuff? You probably had all sorts of notes from me in your desk, bleep bleep bleep... Oh, <u>BLLLLLEEEEEEP!</u> I really hope you got rid of that one about Noah Spivak... you know which one I mean. Oh God! I really hope you destroyed it!!!!! Please, Anjali, you need to tell me that you did or else I am totally going to die of humiliation.

AAAAAAAAAAAAAAAAAAAAAAAAAAAAAAAAAAAAAAAAAAAA

of course I guess the upside of dying of humiliation is that we'll be reunited soon.

later

In English now. I think you must've destroyed that note or else someone else did because apparantly Noah Spivak has not read it. He just came in and sat down at the desk right <u>in front of me which</u> might be a first

I mean like in all the years I've been going to school with

him Noah Spivak has never said anything to me beyond hey but now he keeps looking backward like he wants to tell me something

when he looks back he looks strangely sad, which makes me feel like I know something about him

when he looks away from me I get this view of this freakle he has on the back of his neck and that's wierd too because that's something else I know about him, something he probably doesn't know himself

I am staring

staring

staring at that freakle

everyone else is staring at me

it's like they're waiting to see if I'm going to start crying or something

I bet they'd like that but I won't—

It's not just that I'm not one of those criers but also because crying's what you do when you stub your toe real hard or bite your tongue when you're eating beef jerky it is entirely insufficient when your best friend unreasonably ups and DIES

What I'm doing is something else entirely.

What I'm doing is what the earth does when there's no rain and the grass is dried up and silent cracks spread across the dying land

that's me

and when Noah Spivak turns around to look at me he won't catch me crying

he'll just see the tumbleweeds blowing across the parched parched ground

BEEEEEP! That wasn't me swearing as you can tell if you read closely

That was the bell

thank god

I thought this period would never end

English may be my favorite class but sometimes that's not saying much

Anjali!!!!!!!!!

Where are you? I need you to be here so I can tell you how much I hate Wendy Mathinson!!!!!!!!!!!!!!!!!!!! a thousand times!!

I hate her

I detest and loathe and despise and abore and abominate her

She is a BLEEEEEP

And when I say BLEEEEP I mean the worst kind ever

She is all the bad words I know

on top of that she is all the bad words I don't know and maybe even the ones that have not yet been invented

You'd think since my best friend just DIED D-I-E-D DIEDIEDIEDIED she could give me a break for 45 seconds or so just now I left my book on the table and she touched it before she knew it was mine

then she was screaming like I was a leper and there was lepersy all over the book and her arms and legs were going to start falling off or something

I wish they would!

I hate her

I hate her

I hates her forever

December 22

Sorry it's been so long since I wrote, Anjali—I've just been so busy that I forgot all about you.

Joke! Joke! Jokeing. You know I'm never going to forget you. It's still November 16th and I am still trapped in school with Wendy Mathinson. I'm so tired of it. So tired of November 16th. Why is it still November 16th, Anjali???? November 16th is going on FOREVER!!!!!!! It's just going on and on, and I don't know if I can stand it here without you at home

ridiculously still November 16

Oh God Anjali save me from November 16th

now I'm back home but it's not much better

mostly I've spent the afternoon lying on my bed

staring staring staring at the cieling like I did

all last week instead of going to school

sometimes I vary the programme by gazing at

the door but that in reality is very depressing

because it makes me think about the way the door

opened the night you died

AAAAAAAAAAAAAAAAAAAAAAAAAAAAAAAH

I hate remembering it but still I can't help each

time I look at that door

The memory is very vivid

I was just sitting on my bed trying to read

while Katie jabbered away on the cellphone she got for her 16th birthday jabbering jabbering jabbering giggle giggle jibber my swwet LORD she never STOPS

I was rereading the same passage for like the millionth time when I heard my mother come shuffling up the stairs

There was something about that shuffling that made me pause even though it is a very familiar sound.

As long as I can remember my mother has been dragging her feet while she walks

That is what I alwsys say about her: Marilyn Beals walks on her heels.

This time the scuffling sounded very reluctant

it sounded so reluctant it made me stop reading and sit up

I turned my head and saw the handle turn

it tuuuuuuuuuuurned very slowly

(I knew something was wrong but i didn't yet get how very wrong it was) and then my mother came in and everything was different forever.

"Katie," she said in a sad and quiet voice. "Kay-Kay, please--I need to talk to Meredith alone."

"Why? What did she do?" asked Katie eagerly.

"Nothing," my mother pleaded. "Come on, Kay. Please take the phone somewhere else."

"Can I go in your room?"

"Fine, fine," my mother agreed. "Wherever. But GO, Katie."

Katie flounced off her bed. When she got near me, she put the phone up to her chest.

"What did you do, anyway?" she hissed. I didn't know--I couldn't think of anything. But still I felt a great nervous weight pressing on me.

My mother closed the door as Katie left and leaned against it heavily. She's not particularly small but she was dwarfed by that door as she stood there opening and closing her mouth like a fish that unexpectedly finds itself drowning on land.

Watching her made me realize how hard it was for me to breathe myself

i had to keep remembering to draw in another breath as she stood there trying and trying to start

"Meredith--"

and

"Meredith, honey--"

and

"Meredith, sweetie--"

and finally

"Oh, May-May, it's Anjali."

"What about Anjali!!!!" I demanded, terrified, but still I didn't know.

"Oh, Meredith--Chandra just called. Anjali went into the hospital this morning, with a fever and... oh, honey... it was ensephilitis. They couldn't do anything for her... she..."

"No," I informed her.

"Sweetie, sweetie, it's so awful, but it's true. She d... she passed away."

Remember how we talked about that, how dumb it is when people say "passed away" or "passed on" or "gone"? Usually my mother is not like that as you know she is always insisting on saying Bowel Movement or B.M. in a very embarasing way which drives me CrAzY but now she couldn't make herself say the real words and then I GOT it because I couldn't make myself hear them either.

"No," I said again, shaking my head.

My mother was crying. "I can't believe it," she said, as if to herself. "I can't believe she;s gone. Her poor mother."

"No," I said for the third time, but she just looked at me very sorrowfully and asked me if I wanted to be alone.

NO!!!!! I wanted to shout NO I **NEVER WANTED TO BE ALONE** but apparantly the universe was not listening because it had just made me entirely and like FOREVER alone by taking you away from me but my mother apparantly misunderstood what I was feeling because she kissed me and quietly closed the door behind her. After awhile I got up and locked it. I'm not supposed to do that, but then again you're not supposed to die either so I guess it all evens out.

That was when I called Noah Spivak but after that disaster I sat still for a long time. Finally I got up and took out the necklace we got at the Topsfield Fair in October. Do you remember that necklace? I wore my half of it for a couple of weeks after until it started turning my neck green and my mother made me take it off. I don't know what you did with your half. I never wondered that before because the necklace wasn't important before you died--it was just a dumb joke, like we were 10 or something and all Best Friends Forever.^{TM} Still it was kind of fun to get our names engraved on it, even if they did spell my name wrong

Remember how it took us a ridiculously long time to figure out which of us would get each half? At first you said you'd take the BEST AR FOR side because it was worse--you said I was nicer to you than you were to me so I should get the good side for once. But then you changed your mind and said I should take the bad side for the very reason that I was so nice that i would be willing to take it

you smiled when you said it and I wanted to make you happy so I gave you the FRIENDS E EVER side and handed the other one to the man to misspell my name on.

I remember everything about that night

we went up the on the Ferris wheel with the necklaces around our necks looking at the world below, seeing things we;d never seen before sort of like that time we got up on that chair and realized your uncle is in point of fact bald

"Do you think we really will be best friends forever?" you then suddenly asked.

"Of course we'll be best friends forever," I said. "Why wouldn't we be best friends forever? That's stupid talk."

"Chandra isn't speaking to her best friend any-more," you said. "They fought."

"About what?" I asked.

"About a boy," you said.

"Well, the boys will always like you best, so there won't be anything for us to fight about," I said.

"It wasn't that," you said back. "They fought because Chandra liked a boy and she didn't spend that much time with Nancy anymore."

"Well," I told you. "I just won't let you do that. I'll just follow right behind you and Noah Spivak. You'll be up on the Ferris wheel like this, and he'll be like, why is this car tipping so much, and you'll be like, oh, that's just Meredith Beals weighing it down."

"No," you said, shaking your head. "It won't be like that at all. I'll be like, move over, Noah, Meredith needs a place to sit."

"So we'll be best friends forever?" I asked you.

"Forever," you said.

"Richer or poorer?"

"In sickness or health."

"To death do us part?"

"Nah," you said. "Nah, even after death. Why should we stop being friends just because one of us is dead? That's dumb. We'll be best friends FOREVER, Meredith Beals, not just until one of us dies, and you can put that in the bank and write a check on it."

"What does that mean?" I asked you.

"I don;t know," you said. "It's just something my father says. I guess it just means that whoever dies first will have to hang around and haunt the other one."

And we held the two broken parts of the necklace together, so that it said

BEST FRIENDS

ARE

FOREVER

and we rocked the Ferris wheel car some more.

So that's what I've been thinking lately, Anjali, about how you said FOREVER. I'm holding you to it, too, because otehrwise I really can't handle it that you're dead.

M.

November 17

Dear Anjali,
   WHERE ARE YOU? Are you drifting around like a ghost in the rain? I'm sitting here in English and staring out the scratched plastic windows and it's looking very ghostly outside and dreary too with the mist and the drizzle and wonderi
   Anjali!!!!!!!
Did you see that????????????
   that's the second time it happened—I looked up and Noah Spivak was STARING in this direction
   THERE! Again! And also now!
   Now the back of my neck is prickling because I am wondering if someone is standing behind me
   (is it you, Anjali???)
   WIERD
   there's the bell
   maybe when I leave class he'll say something

He didn't say anything to me. Duh. As if.

I'm home now but it's not much better than school bcause my **BLEEPING** sister is downstairs complaining to our mother that I am leaving PAPER all over our room as if that is a CRI**M**E

I can hear her now clomping around the kitchen in her big stupid CLOGS like she is a little dutch boy sticking her finger in a hissy fit

now she is proclaiming that my typing is like little nails to her **SKULL** and asking the heavens why I can;t use a computer like a Normal Human Being^{TM}

she just doesn't get it that I feel closer to you when I type on the typewriter

the computer is just too digital for our commu-
nications the words are not REAL/but the typerwriter is a very physical thing kind of like life
and death.

Besides I just like it.

it makes me write in the Heming way

you could not write "The Old Man and the Sea"
on a computer any more than Shakspere could've
written Hamlet on a typerwriter

ooops now my mother is shuffling up the stairs
shuffle scuffle slip shuffle here she is shuffling in

out with the paper zzoooop on with the innocent
look gleeeeee

Back. Poor, poor, Katie that she doesn't
have a dead best friend. Now she doesn't get
her Princess^{TM} way because everyone has to be
nice to me hah hahahaha it's about time let me
tell you

it was actually kind of funny

my mother was revealing that she is concerned about my MENTAL HEALTH because she
has returned to using our baby nicknames which
is something she only does when she is worried
we are about to fly off the handle.

"May-May," she said, "Kay-Kay is feeling
frustrated that your side of the room is getting
a little...STREWN."

Haha hah "STREWN" is one word for it. My mis-
sives and epistles to you are kind of EVERYWHERE

"So she was wondering when you were going to
clean it up?" (rising tone at the end of the sentence signaling tentativeness--Pritchard taught
me that)

(Also Pritchard informs me tentativeness sig-
nals weakness which is why We Girls must be on
the Look Out for it and Not Do That Rising Tone
Thing EVER but in this case I took advantage
of the signaled weakness and made my Custard's
Last Stand even though I know Katie always gets
her way:

"I'll clean up the letters when I know Anjali's read them."

Then my mother suprized me. Usually I can predict everything she will do but sometimes I am wrong because this time she sat down very suddenly on my bed.

"You're leaving these papers here for Anjali?" she asked in a sad, heavy sort of voice.

"Yeah," I answered. "I mean, it wasn't like she left a forwarding adress."

That made my mother a little teary. She is very sentimental unlike me

I am made of **ROCK**

I might be a ROBOT actually though lately my program has gotten a bit wiggy and sometimes I get a little teary though i usually am opposed to that sort of thing as you know

Now I have a new stradegy: when I think I'm going to cry I touch our necklace. I still haven't taken it off since the day you died and i will not take it off until my neck turns so GREEN that my

HEAD FALLS OFF from the gangreen and that is my promise to you Anjali Sen which you can take to the bank and write a check on

"But how will you know when Anjali's read the letters?" my mother asked at last.

Here's the thing: I didn't have an answer to that. How will I know, Anjali? Don't you think it's about time for you to give me a sign, like you promised? What part of best friends **FOREVER** do you not understnad?

Your best friend,

Meredith

P.S. Katie's back schlumping prissily around. You're so lucky you got Chandra for a sister instead of Katie "I am a Princess of Perfection^{TM}" Beals. Can you imagine Katie calling YOU if I was the one who died? She'd probably call all her friends first and then all the people she doesn't even like, and she'd be like "OMIGOD you would not believe

what **HAPPENED!** My spazzy sister went and **DIED!**
I know!" and they'd shriek and carry on at the stupid thing I'd gone and done and maybe only 3 days
later she might get around to caring that my best
friend might want to know that I was dead.

P.S.S. I think Katie read that last bit. She snorted something
at me when she was coming to bed. Well, BLEEP you, too,
Katie!!!!! Everything I said about you was true, and all the
things I haven't said are true, too, like this: I wish it was you
who was dead, not Anjali.

Now it's 1:15 at night. I feel really bad I said that about Katie. Now I'm sitting up
watching her because I'm scared she might suddenly stop breathing and then it will be
my fault. Don't die, Katie! Anjali doesn't want to be stuck with you in heaven while she
waits around for me.

Nov. 18 I think

anyway it's Wednesday

Dear Anjali,

I really really hate it that you're dead. It's worst
after school. I'm really not sure what I'm supposed to
do with myself for all those hours. Yesterday afternoon Colette Soulier invited me over to hang out with
her and her sister Laurel but I didn't really feel
like it but then today when I thought I might want to
go she didn't say anything. I guess it didn't matter
because I had this doctor appointment at 4:30 anyway but still it would've been nice to be asked

I'm supposed to see this doctor every Wednesday
to help me sort out my Feelings^{TM}

My mother says he's very expensive which I SHOULDN'T WORRY ABOUT but on the other hand she wants me to take it seriously and not just moodily stare at the wall as I am Apt to Do but rather take advantage of his Expert-Ease^{TM}

As far as I am concerned that is very cruddy so I asked her how long I have to see him

she said I should go until I feel better which means that this Dr. Martin is going to be taking alot of my parents' money to the bank and writing checks on it because I am not really thinking I will be feeling better any time soon especially because of that Wendy BLEEPING Mathinson

I hate her so MUCH!!!!!! This afternoon it was worst

After my stupid appointment with stupid Dr. Martin I found myself stupidly drifting over toward your house

I sat there on the stoop like I was waiting for you to come down to me

it's not that I don't get it that you're not going

to come down those stairs again, Anjali--it's just that I don't really get what that means that you're not

Eventually my feet drifted me toward the Gladden playground and I sat on the swings for the longest time. One of the bolts is really loose in the broken one and it's creaking very mournfully

(I tell you Anjali one of these days that chain's going to fall down on somebody and that will really cause a commotion)

Anyway I was sitting there not bothering anyone AT ALL and suddenly there's Wendy Mathinson standing there and cackling at me the BLEEP standing cackling hah haha "What are you doing there, Beals, can't you READ? It says **NO DOGS ALLOWED!**" cackling cackling cackling like the evil WITCH that she is

WHY CAN'T I GET AWAY FROM HER????

I really wish I was good at that comeback thing so I could say something to her like oh HA HA

WENDY YOU **ARE** SUCH **A WIT** or at least something that ryhmes with it!!!!!

ARGH!!!!!! I really can;t tell you how much I hate her

I'll say this again Anjali: Wendy Mathinson might be pretty and she might be popular and she might be all DEVELOPED and all but she is still a DRIED PIECE OF SNOT. She is EAR WAX. She is the peeling SKIN between your TOES that gets so mixed up with CRUD you don't even know what it is anymore. She is PUS. She is the STINKY ROTTEN PUS that comes out of a pimple when you squeeze it she is a BLEEP of the worst kind a B.M. one and she will be one forever and you can put THAT in the bank and write a check on it. Why does she even need to even talk to me? Stupid barking pimple snot pus bowel **BLEEEEP!!!!** Why can't I get away from her????

Back when you were around I used to be able to ignore her but now it's impossible. Sometimes I think it's because having you as a friend was like having a cloke of invisibility but now I've lost it because you took it with you when you died.

That wasn't very nice of you Anjali. I really need that cloke

Bow. Wow.

m

P.S. I wish I really was a dog. If I was I would bite Wendy Mathinson on the leg.

THURSDAY. This is ridiculous. I'm in Media where I am supposed to be doing research online about the Micmac Indians but I tell you Anjali I do not need to know about the Micmac at this moment in time I need to talk to YOU because I need you to tell me what this means:

"Don't bother Meredith, she's okay."

Please tell me! Is that a compliment? An insult? Really, Anjali, what would you think, if someone said that about you? Please answer soon because I am really wondering

BLEEP here comes Wilson

[delete]

[delete]

BLEEEEEEEEEEEEEEEEEEEEEEEEEEEEP!!! Wilson caught me not searching about the Micmac Indians and thought I was doing email instead which is ridiculous as I have no one to email to unless you count my grandmother and believe me I'm not in such a desperate rush to be communicating with her

Now she thinks I didn't do any work AT ALL and gave me detension, the BLEEEEEEP. How is that going to teach me about the Micmac I ask you????? and besides and more importantly I still don't know what THIS means:

DON'T BOTHER MEREDITH—SHE'S OKAY

Let me try to tell you what happened

I was coming through the front door this morning and there were all those kids on that bench in front of the plants next to the water fountain

I tell you Anjali I don't know why all those plants are

there unless they are supposed to make you think you are drinking from a clean and pristine jungle spring but I tell you when you see Wendy Mathinson and that boy Zev and the rest of them sitting there it's more like you've stumbled upon an EVIL OASIS and there's Wendy in the middle of it poisoning the water supply and barking at me ha ha she is such a bleeping ZIT

But here's the wierd thing: suddenly in the middle of all that EVIL there is a voice saying, "Aw Wendy cut it out."

That was very unusual but what was even more very unusual was that it was NOAH SPIVAK'S voice + then he stood up from amongst the green and growing plants saying:

"Don't bother Meredith. She's okay."

Wendy's EVIL face got all white and green.

"HER?" she said, quite wittily in my opinion. But then Noah Spivak, NOAH SPIVAK said, "Yeah, HER," and then to me (to me, this is actual ME I'm talking about) he said, "See ya around, Meredith." And he sauntered away.

And now you know the whole story, everything I know about it, and I know everything about it except this:

WHAT DOES IT MEAN???????

Now I still have to go to stupid detension and sit there and stare at the wall thinking what does it mean what does it mean what does it mean what does it mean

Now I'm here in detension
still thinking
Don't bother Meredith, she's okay.
???
???
I don't get it forward
let's try it backward
Yako sehs htiderem rehtob t'nod
that looks like Hebrew
Noah Spivak studies Hebrew
but
Anjali
Anjali!!
Anjali talk to me!!!!!
you can't pretend you're not there

that must be you there pulling the strings

How did you do it? How did you get Noah Spivak in detension with me?????? because he's coming through the door!!!!!!!

He's over there right over THERE looking at me at me
at ME

(sorry about the echo I'm a little flabberflummoxed)

He keeps looking when he thinks I'm not looking at him

of course I'm looking at him pretty much all the time

I have been looking at him for several years now really

I know you have suggested that he is (Way) Out of My
League

I know and have accepted that he is (Way) Out of My
League, which is why I told you that of course you should
get to be the one to like him but still Anjali I have to say it
again: that Noah Spivak is kind of cute

later

ANJALI!!!!!!!!!!!!!!!!!!!!!!!!!!!

You must've seen it

you must've been there

I could feel you there making it happen

you must;ve seen the note he passed me!!!!!

I have preserved it and here it is

HEY MEREDITH!
WHAT'S WORSE THAN FINDING A WORM IN
YOUR APPLE? FINDING HALF A WORM

I was not really sure how to answer that

I think I was sick that day in Human

Relationships when they talked about what to do when the boy you might like passes you a very lame joke like that

    I was forced to wing it

this is a **reproduction of my reply**

Hey Noah

what happened at the hockey game at the leper colony

there was a face-off in the corner hahahahhahaha

here is his response

THAT'S NOT NICE

HAHAHAHA ANYWAY

HEY MEREDITH WHAT'S WORSE THAN FINDING

HALF A WORM IN YOUR APPLE

my reconstructed reply

????

then he said this

HAVING RUSTY SPIKES NAILED INTO YOUR HEAD

that was when I laughed too much in detension and got sent to see Walsh instead

she did not even think the joke was funny which proves once and for all what I always say about her though she was a little nicer than I anticipated

she spoke semi-sympathetically about your demise but reminded me that is not an excuse for me to slack off indefinitely

she said she would forgive the 5 days staring at the cieling but emphasized she does not want to see me in detension again and especially not getting detension in detension which is really delinquent

(next thing you know I will get in trouble in Walsh's office after getting kicked out of detension and then they will probably have to send me to jail or something)

Anyway I was not so much paying attention to her speaking since I was still a little intrigued by the whole Noah Spivak passing me notes thing finally the late bell rang and Walsh let me go and I gathered up my stuff and came into the main hallway.

Let me set the scene for you:

For the eyeball setting: the empty hall.

For the nostril setting: Mr. Clean

For the eardrum setting: me clonking through the hall

(and also the echoes coming clonking back

back

back)

back to the eyeballs: movement down the hall--

someone is standing

it's him

it is

it's

N! O! A! H! S! P! I! V! A! K!

sitting or so it seems **WAITING** on that bench next to the planter

Wendy Mathinson's evil aura still SHIMMERS there but otherwise it is a beneficient oasis because Noah Spivak is waiting there #alone# looking like he is waiting for *ME*

(and while that seems highly unlikely it still really seems that way)

I am falling

I am flailing

I don't know what to do

the hall is getting loooooooooooooooooooooonger as I stand there it is like some special effect it is ssstttrrreeeeetchhhhing out

(I think I want to run away but it's like Noah Spivak has me in his tractor beams)

I am having a hard time laying my mind o nthe word HELLO which is usually rather accessable but not when you are ME and **NOAH SPIVAK** is staring at you

now he is coming closer

he is speaking

the words come to me from underwater

time is like a record that is s

l

o

w

i

ng down and

then **NOAH SPIVAK** is saying

"Hey Meredith sorry about Walsh."

(time speeding up again going faster than usual
I might get thrown clear of the earth as I hear
him say the next words)

"Don't you live near Gladden? Cause I was walking that way too...."

WAGGA WAGGA WAGGA BOING

I needed a moment to process that

!!

even after that long moment I needed another
one because I am dizzy with the world spinning off
it's axis I mean I never really thought I'd hear
Noah Spivak wanting to talk to ME I mean like I
told you I always thought he'd want to talk to YOU

Anjali but to me MEREDITH not so much

so I'm sitting there going !!!!!!!!!!!!!! and BO-ING!

and then I realize: I've been waiting for a sign all this time that you;re still with me, and now this totally wierd thing has happened, and that makes me think that you must've had something to do with it, right????? because now I'm leaving the school with Noah Spivak Noah SPIVAK and he's asking me if you told me that leper joke and I'm telling him about my Uncle Paul who is a professional writer of books of gross jokes that are shaped like toilets

and he's asking me how jokes can be shaped like toilets and then I'm kind of having to hit him on the shoulder. (Are you listening, Anjali? I had to kind of hit NOAH SPIVAK)

and then I'm cursing my parents that they moved so close to the school because though it is usually an annoying treck our feet are now eating up all the last yards and inches and then this moment is going to be over and there's Gladden

and there's your house

(I look up and see your bedroom window with the shade mostly drawn and then I feel a little melanchaly)

(for a moment I can imagine you peeking out from under the shade and seeing me there with Noah Spivak)

(and then for a moment I can imagine me peeking out from under the shade and seeing YOU there with him, and that makes me very glad I never had to see that because even though I did say you could like him I'm not sure I could've handled that

but now it's ME Meredith walking home with him

Still I don't think you should be jealous Anjali I mean because well you know

anyway at that moment Noah Spivak looks up where I'm looking and then he says,

"that was her house, wasn't it?"

I nod, and he says,

"You must really miss her."

That is a funny thing.

People say that to me ALL THE TIME They say it so often the words have worn little holes in my EAR DRUMS with their speaking but now Noah Spivak's saying it and it's like no one ever noticed before how much I miss you.

It must've been the way he said it

sometimes I think people are saying it to make fun of me but in the mouth of Noah Spivak it sounded like an invitation and so I began to speak

I started talking about the first day,

the first day we met right there at the Gladden playground

the day I peeked out at you from behind my mother's stockinged legs (and I still remember the way the run in her stockings looked)

then you peeked out at me from behind your mother's stockinged legs (and I still can remember the way your face looked from behind her brightly colored pants) then very s h y l y we started playing in the sandbox

my mother said we cried when they made us stop playing, and that we never stopped playing since.

she said it was love at first sight, that's what my mother said, but I didn't tell Noah Spivak that part because he might of thought I meant like IN LOVE love but that's not what she meant at all. She meant LOVE like the love you're supposed to have for sisters only I had it for you instead of for Katie

I told Noah Spivak how my mother said we never did stop playing after that first day.

we played from that first moment in the sandbox until the last day we played Spit in your kitchen and you kept getting the Stinky King over and over because like we said the boys always liked you best.

(and now we're sitting on the creaky creaky Gladden swings and Noah Spivak is just listening)

I'm talking about what an honor it was to be your friend when you were so funny so smart so nice so pretty then he said something nice about you

and I said some more nice things about you

and then he said he wanted to learn to play Spit

so he could feel closer to you

WAGGA WAGGA BOING!

SO **THAT'S WHAT I'VE BEEN SPENDING THIS
LETTER WAITING TO SAY TO YOU:**

NOAH SPIVAK IS COMING OVER TOMORROW

AFTERNOON SO WE CAN TEACH HIM TO PLAY

SPIT!!!!!!!!!!!!

we = you and I, I mean, because of course you

should be there with me to teach him

In my opinion you should always be there with me

(or maybe not ALL the time

I do like a little privacy in the bathroom you know)

                    Meredith

P.S. Can I repeat something??????? N.S. wants to come over and learn how to play SPIT tomorrow!!! !!!!!!. ¡¡¡¡¡

P.S.S. Hey Anjali I hope you're not feeling jealous or anything that Noah Spivak's coming over tomorrow

in all likelihood he just wants to learn to play Spit because in point of fact he's desperately in love with YOU

P.S.S.S. But even if Noah's just wants to come over because he's desperately in love with YOU, that still must mean he doesn't totally hate ME, doesn't it?

Friday November 20th

homeroom

I have to tell you Anjali it was very wierd walking to school this morning and thinking about meeting Noah Spivak

I mean I was almost even feeling a little happy which was odd as these days I am more used to feeling miserably sad

I mean it's just WIERD knowing that after all these years he knows and I know and I know HE knows and I know HE knows that I know HE knows that we're going to leave school TOGETHER in like 6 hours which has never happened before

it's like I've jumped into a different reality

some people say it's like that

they say there are billions of universes with a billion versions of each life

most of them are pretty similar I guess

everything the same except a little cough here or there
or the choosing of vanilla instead of chocolate

but then again little decisions might make for big changes

like for example the reality where your parents took you
to the hospital a little earlier

Anyway

now there's only like 5 hours and 36 minutes left

Dear Anjali--

Back home.

Should I tell you about my day?

I know you want me to.

I feel you there leaning in and looking to see
what letter I am going to put down next

I feel you trying to hurrrrrrry me along to get
to the PO**INT** like you used to say

maybe you're even trying to finish my sentences
wherever you are but I will defy you by writing
random manglewurzle hahahah

so you remember I last left you in homeroom
waiting waiting for the day to be over

I had not seen Noah yet but I knew when I did
he would be knowing as I was knowing that we

were both knowing that we were going to spend the afternoon together

that's what I was thinking in MATH

that's what I was thinking in SCIENCE

but then as I was going to SPANISH suddenly I realized something, e.g.

YO SOY LOCA

YO SOY COMPLETEMENTE LOCA

obviously I was hallucinating yesterday

I mean why would NOAH SPIVAK want to hang out with fat ugly me??? I mean it is totally CRAZY to think he would want to come over to my house after school it is LOCISIMO

I knew I was CRAZY when I walked through the lunch room

in a crazy way I had sort of thought we might eat together but then I saw him at a table with that boy Adam who might be a jerk and that guy Zev who really is one and when I saw him I knew for sure there was no way NOAH SPIVAK would want to hang out with me this afternoon

I just walked by him face burning and sat down
to eat my lonely meatloaf and isolated peas

God i hate lunch

i didn't used to hate it despite the inferior
food because you were there with me and I didn't
feel that spotlight shining on me a blinking neon
light with one broken letter flickering over my
head **ALO E ALO E ALO E**

(GOD Anjali I really need my cloke of invisibility back it really wasn't fair for you to take it away)

I look over and Noah Spivak's just eating eating eating the so-called food and ignoring me
and there's Wendy coming through the lunch line
squeeeeeeeeeeeeeezing through the narrow space
next to the cash register because someone's taking too long choosing desert (they should really do
something about that badly designed location) and
then Noah's watching as she sashays EVILLY across
the room and sits down with him and Adam and Zev

(ahhhhh)

the meatloaf has turned to sawdust in my mouth

the peas are balls of lead I'm going to choke

but then Noah stands up

and

(ah?)

(now he's walking over with his cloudy green eyes)

now he's walking towards me!

(now past me)

going

to

buy

desert

(aaaaaaaaaaaaaaaaaaaaaaaaaaaaah that is
the sound of my heart deflating as it is pierced
with a shard of misery)

(actually I'm serious it was quite depressing)

I am deflated like a broken balloon

I can hardly drag myself out of the stupid
lunch room

I am dragging my deflated self through the halls

and Anjali it seems too much to bear that I have
gym next

I mean going to English is not so bad when you're depressed because many of the stories you read there are a little melanchalay

besides there is always the chance you will get to write a pome to ExPrEsS your FeeLiNgS

Math is also okay because numbers are sort of emotion-neutral but gym is awful

just walking into that sweaty room can make me feel lousy.

I tell you this Anjali, we were wrong when we used to say gym was unbareable

it was actually a little bareable, as long as you were there with me.

Now I told Morgan-Mack that I was feeling too sad to play basketball. I think she's alot nicer now that she's Morgan-Mack and not just Mack. She didn;t give me a Mack Attack at all but just let me go to the nurse. Maybe getting married does that to a person, I don't know. Anyway then I was dragging myself to the nurse very sslloowwllyyyyyyy

that Greatful Dead song "Box of Rain" was

playing on the radio when I came into the office and I felt very moody because it was like I was at your house listening to "American Beauty." If I had that CD I could listen to it while I lied on my bed and thought of you

A BOX OF RAIN WILL EASE THE PAIN

AND LOVE WILL SEE YOU THROUGH

****that was a musical interlude****

And then... while I was lying on the hard purple cot... just as the bell rang... in comes... you're not going to believe it...

"Hey!" says Noah Spivak, his voice all crinkly with concern. "Are you okay? I saw you leaving the gym...."

I had to scramble up then, because it's really embarasing to be lying down in front of someone, and when I did I kind of choked on my own spit and had this coughing fit. (That was also embarasing if you want to know the truth).

Noah looked at my choking to death and objected to it.

"But..." he protested, "but... I thought we were going to hang out together this afternoon..."

!!

oingo boingo

That was when I managed to stop coughing and clue him into the faking-to-get-out-of-gym thing and the choking-on-my-own-spit thing and then Noah Spivak smiled at me

hello, sparkling cloudy green eyes

hello, wrinkled up freakled nose

hello Noah Spivak who I have liked since like 5th grade

"So you'll still meet me after school?" he asked.

"Where?"

"Like near the rock over on Marrett?"

That was a little *ouch*--that meant he didn't want to meet me right next to school but I guess it was a mercy not to have to deal with Wendy Mathinson and the rest of the snot rags but still ((ouch).) But what am I going to say?

let me give you a multiple choice quiz

a) yes.

So I met him after school, Anjali, I really did. There I am after school crunching across the frosted grass to meet him

my toes are crackling through the puddles of white ice in the big field and I can see him waiting on the rock

he is waiting there for ME M**EREDITH J. BEALS** and that is a sentence I could never write before. !!!!!

It was a)#@*GREAT*@#(afternoon

mostly we talked about the fact that everyone at school wants to talk about you even if they didn't know you (and when I say everyone I am not just mispelling "one or two people")

they all want to know someone who's died, even those people who think your name is pronounced Ann-ja-lee and not Ahn-juh-lee

but even though I hate to hear them talking about you when they didn't know you it is worse that sometimes there are days when no one mentions you at all. That makes me panick, as if you are slipping away from the world like Kristi Lawrence did after she drownded. Remember that? We talked about her and talked about her and then we forgot to talk about her and then it was like she had slipped through the ice for a second time with the black waters closing over her again and then she was gone forever.

But I won't let that happen to you Anjali I WON'T and Noah says he won't either and he'll help me keep you here with me.

He GETS it that telling pointless stories about the Stinky King is an important way to bind you here to me and that's what we talked about as we waited for everyone to leave so we could go home

I have to say Anjali it was very strange to talk TO Noah Spivak after all those years of talking ABOUT him. Actually I was thinking it's kind of funny that we liked him so much when we didn't know him at all. Why did we like him, when we'd never even talked to him? Was it just because he's so cute? I hope we're not that sHaLloW but maybe

(Can you believe
this is page 10 of
this letter
i am very prolific)

we were. Because it's wierd how liking a person is not a very national I mean rational thing it's more like you've got no choice in the matter

But anyway

Being with Noah Spivak talking about you is a little bit like being with YOU talking about Noah Spivak

it's like he was always with us then, but invisible

and now it's like you're here with us, but invisible

but then anyway we came to my house and I taught let me repeat that I **TAUGHT NOAH SPIVAK** how to play Spit

we played at the table just like you used to do with me

he drank milk just like you used to do with me

i let him win just like I used to do with you hah ha

(Actually he did win which was a little embarasing for me but then again maybe you were hel-
ping him--he said he might've felt you doing that)

we sat there for a long time smacking at the cards
with me kind of getting to know the real Noah Spivak

he's not quite the way we thought he would be

He is goofier and also a little sentimental but I
am not complaining

all in all it was a fairly amazing afternoon but
I am too sleeeeeepy now tow rite moer

Also I am kind of intrigued as to who might be
in my dreams tonight

                         Your best friend,
                         Meredith

P.S. Aren't you impressed I wrote you such a
LOOOOONG letter?

November 21

Saturday and no school thank god i can sit here
all day and write all about Noah Spivak

where shall we start?

with his EYES that are like the green sea
reflecting a brooding sky

or his TEETH which are very intriguing (for
some reason braces are enhancing on him as they
draw attention to his pouted mouth)

or maybe

!!.

that 2 and 1/2 exclamation points was how long
it took Katie to pounce on the phone

whenever the phone rings she acts just like

a cat running when you open a can of something, even if it's not tunafish

sorry kitty katie this time it was not tuna because the phone was for

ME!

(hard to believe I know but it was)

Katie held out the reciever very disdainfully and said it was some boy calling

I took the call in my parent's room

I will leave you in suspense as to who it was calling but while you're guessing I'll tell you this: we are going out to drink cofee at Dunkin' Donuts so see you later Anjaleeeee

later

Anjali do I seem different to you? I drank my first cup of cofee today, but it wasn't all that good. In my opinion it tastes a little bit like death but I guess death is okay with alot of milk and alot of sugar. (There may be a lesson there).

Noah is a big cofee drinker

That is because it turns out he's going to be a MAN in 3 months

Jewish people are very mature apparantly

that is because in Hebrew he's not 12 he's 21 hhahahha

he's going to have this big ceremony when he turns 13

he says I can go if I like although it is likely to be gnirob (that is Hebrew for boring in case you did not know because they are a little sdrawkcab over there).

The funny thing was that there was this cup on the counter that said TIPS on it where you were supposed to put your change and Noah said that it was a good thing we weren't in Isreal because then everyone would think they were supposed to spit into it hahahahahaha

then we went back to my house and into the kitchen to play Spit

I told him if we were in Isreal we'd have to

play Tips instead hahhahahahha

We played a long time and this time I beat him and he said he wanted a rematch but it was late and tomorrow he is going to the movies with Zev and Adam

I wanted to ask if Wendy was going to go too but luckily I managed to stop myself before the words snuck out because when it comes down to it I didn't really want to know. That is one thing that confuses me about Noah, that he does not seem to recognize that Wendy Mathinson has LEPERSY OF THE SOUL and sometimes it makes me nervously wonder why he is spending all this time with me. I mean I know all about not putting the gift horse before the cart and all and especially because I sort of think you might of had a hand in his coming over I'm not going to question it but still:

what does it all mean, Anjali?

Merrydith

Sunday

November Somethingth

I guess it is very churchy of me but now I'm spending this Sabbath wondering where in the name of
all that's holy you are

WHERE ARE YOU, ANJALI???

Now it's the 2 week birthday of your death and
I've been lying on my bed for the past hour thinking about this question and concluding that you
must be SOMEWHERE because if there's the conversation of mass and the conversation of energy like
they talk about in Science then there has to be a
conversation of YOU because you are more important than any stupid mass or any stupid energy!

So WHERE are you??? You are GRavely Mistaken if
you don't think I need some proof re: your where-
abouts and I don't mean that as a joke. It's really
not funny. Really!!!!!!!

It's not that I;ve never gone this long without
you. We were separated longer that summer you drove
across the country and it's true I did manage to sur-
vive those 5 weeks without you. I remember how much
I dreaded your going--the only way I could stand
it was to write all those letters to you beforehand
so you could read them on your trip. I wrote to you
every day when you were gone too because I didn't so
much have anything else to do and besides writing
to you made me feel like you were a little bit with
me. And then each night my mother let me cross off
the day on the big calandar on the kitchen.

It's different now. Now there's no day that you're
going to be coming home, and if I cross out the
days it's like a long line of Xs that marches on
and on almost like it's getting further away from
the place where you and I were together

Except that it's not, not at all, because you promised, you PROMISED that you wouldn't leave me, right, Anjali????? You remember that, don't you????? YOU PROMISED!!! YOU PROMISED ME!!!!!!!

I try to do my part, too

I mean I have promised I will write EVERY DAY for EVER and that is a promise you can take to the bank and write checks on

Also I have promised I will wear our BEST AR FOR necklace until I get neck gangreen, and all these are promises that I have kept. But you have to do your part too, and that means telling me WHERE YOU ARE!!!!!!

I mean come on!! THINK ABOUT IT for a second!!!!

it does not make sense that you could suddenly be GONE.

It doesn't make sense at all.

m

Man Anjali you should've been in school today

(Actually I think you should be in school every day because that would be very preferable to your being dead IMHO)

but you especially should have been there today as you would've been amused

it started in gym when Morgan-Mack requested that Kelly and that DPofS Wendy choose the teams for kickball

you'd think in this day and age they would make a computer program to choose the teams instead of this barbaric ritual that reminds us lepers of our unpopularity in my opinion it would be more efficient

and if the ritual humiliation is all part of the Learning Process^{TM} perhaps the computer could be programed to punch you in the stomach to preserve some of the classic feeling of watching the line around you grow sparser and sparser as you wait to be not-picked next

Eventually I got tired of it.

I mean it was rather obvious that neither of them was going to pick me and that I was going to be last against the wall and then stupid Wendy would be forced to choose me over her objections so in the end I just cut out the middle man and walked over to her group while there were still lots of kids left against the wall

she started shrieking that she hadn't picked me so I explained my reasoning to Morgan-Mack who did not so much appreciate my creative efficiency(of course I don't so much appreciate kick ball so I guess we're even)

Actually I used to really like kick ball back

when we used to play outside without getting a grade on it, back at Gladden when no one barks at you for breaking the no-dog rule or yells at you for missing the ball

now even when you get a run they yell at you for not getting two and then when you have to be pitcher you turn around and suddenly there's no outfield because apparantly Wendy and Nicki went to the bathroom but did not come back

then Eloise said she really really had to go and MM let her which meant our team was down 3 players and then down 5 because Alicia and Arwen left too without even asking and then Morgan-Mack was getting distressed and she left to go find them and then Kelly announced we didn't have to play kick ball anymore and everything kind of degenerated

the funny part was later when Colette Soulier told me that Morgan-Mack found Wendy and all the rest of those girls OUTSIDE text-messaging

I don't know what was so important that it couldn't wait but anyway it doesn't matter because the funny thing is they all lost their cellphones ha ha and also they have week long detension which kind of serves them right because they are not the queens of the world

My mother just came in and commented that I am seeming a little perkier lately.

She asked if it was something that that shrink Martin was telling me that was making me feel better

AS IF!

Personally I think my mother would be better off paying Noah Spivak to make me feel better instead of that dumb Martin

He has a much more salubrious effect on me.

I just learned that word yesterday

it means healthy, I think

or maybe it was salutory that meant healthy I can't really remember

sorry Pritchard

there is a certain freakled distraction in

your class who sometimes makes me pay not so much attention when you are teaching us vocabulareeeeee

   the only problem is that he is sojourning tonight to FLORIDA for Thanksgiving.

   that is kind of a bummer as I was kind of getting used to his company.

                              m

P.S. Hey Anjali--you're not offended that I'm having a good time with Noah Spivak, are you? Because I promise you I am still pretty much entirely miserable.

ANJALI SEN!!!!!!!! GET BACK HERE!!!!!!!!

This is what I need: you

This is why: BLEEPING Wendy Mathinson

I just came out of the stall in the bathroom and there she was

"Oh," she said, all snotty, because that's what she is, a snotty snot snot, "Oh," she says, "<u>THAT'S</u> WHAT THAT SMELL IS."

ha ha HA she is very clever she means me—she is very witty for someone without a BRAIN. You can guarantee that if I was a snot and wanted to go around insulting people I would come up with something better than that like:

"Oh, Wendy, I'm not suprized to see you here, I always think of you when I look in a toilet." Or "There's 2 mirrors here, Wendy—the one you're looking at and the toilet bowl, and they both reflect the same thing." Actually that one's probably a little complicated for her snotforbrains

(later)

It's probably good I didn't say anything. I really wish I was better with the comeback thing. But I wouldn't've NEEDED to say anything if you'd been there because then I would've had my cloke of invisibility instead of being all exposed.

Come ON Anjali!!!! Come back to life already!!!! I need that cloke of invisibility I really do

here's what I **th**ink:

when a person is feeling sad her mother should not make her do things she really doesn't want to do, e.g.: talk to stupid Dr. Martin.

I'm not sure how much I told you about Dr. Martin

I think his name might actually be Dr. Martian

He is a little scary looking

He has hair growing in his ears and a little bit of a halitosis problem

Mostly his main feature is these white puffs of hair above his hairy ears which make him look like Yoda

He is pretty much bald everywhere else though

he does have some elegant long hairs that spring from his eyebrows and a few little corkscrews that come from an evil-looking mole on his chin (I would really have that looked at if I was him)

that is my free verse pome about Mr. Dartin

Ooops! I meant Dr. Martin

Or maybe I didn't

maybe Mr. Dartin is his alter ego or his elter ago or something.

He's really dumb

here's the sort of dumb thing my parents pay him alot of money to say:

"I'm very sorry to hear about your loss."

This is the sort of smart-alex thing I say back:

"Well, I guess my loss is your gain."

Ha ha ha haha haha ha THU MP (that was a witch laughing her head off—that's what passes for humor around here these days)

Dartin said technically what I call humor is actually called deflection and that my parents were spending Good Money for me to be talking about My Feelings instead of avoiding them. I said that if he could teach me to actually avoid My Feelings that might be a good use of my parents' $$$$ as my Feeling of them is actually a bit of a drag. Dartin says that was kind of the cost of being human which is such a crock

I spent most of the 50 minutes staring expensively at the wall.

At least tomorrow is Thanksgiving

At this moment in time I don;t have all that much to be greatful for but I don't mind stuffing my face anyway in honor of people who do

only 12:08 am so it's really like it's still Thanksgiving

Anjali I'm so sorry!!!!!!!!!! I didn't forget to write really

   it's just we didn't eat until really late and then I got all sleepy while we were watching The Sound of Music on TV and I didn't mean to but I fell asleep on the couch and I just woke up

   I really didn't mean to go a whole day without writing

   God it's so scary worrying that if I don't write for a day you'll leave me

Friday Nov 27

I don't know Anjali

I'm feeling a little down today

I guess it's Thanksgiving doing it

I mean I knew you weren't coming over the way you used to all those years when my father would think he was very hilarious from joking that we were like the Pilgrims because we had Indians at our Thanksgiving [ ] <-- that was the sound of me forgetting to laugh

I don't know

I'm just feeling melanchalay.

Katie and I just had this stooopid fight

I had said something about meeting you again in Heaven and she said you wouldn't be there because you're Indian and Hindu and that means you got reincarnated instead

I said that was stupid and you weren't either that you were just normal and she called me a racist for saying Christian is normal

I didn't mean to be racist.

Am I?

later

Now I am a little confused about this reincarnation thing. What does that mean, that you'll come back as someone else? Do you have to come back as a baby? If you do, will you still remember being Anjali? Will you still remember that you were my best friend? And if you don't remember, what's the point? You might as well be dead.

later

Anjali! Anjali!!!!!!!!!

He called!

He's back and he just called!

Are you listening, Anjali R. Sen??????

He C^{A}L$_L$E^D

(I'm a little giddy in case you can't tell)

We had this totally funny conversation and now I'm getting ready to go to the Dunkin' Donuts on Marrett

He said he was going to teach me the Hebrew letters so we can pass secret notes in English or actually in Hebrew hahaha

!nuf

hey anjali do you know now it's many hours later

it's really late and i am feeling too tired to use the shift key

so i went to meet noah at dunkin' donuts

mostly we spent the time talking about you kind of incessantly and then noah wanted to look at some old pictures of you so we came back here which was o.k. though it is not so much actual fun for me to hear him exclaim over and over again how beautiful you were. yes-she-was-really-pretty.

no-she-couldn't-take-a-bad-pitcure-if-she-tried. Go-ahead-shoot-me-now.

9i tell you, anjali, sometimes I wonder how I can stand you in your perfection0

jokelllll

noah stayed for dinner and endeared himself to my mother by complimenting her fried chicken and to my father by laughing at his excessively lame jokes

he didn't have to endaer himself to katie as she is too grown up to spend a friday night with her family that is apparantly for babies you know

goo

anywayy noah just left and i am very tiiiiiiiired

if you were here we wuould turn off the lights now and whisper and giggle all night about him, but as it is i can not tupe any moe beause i am too tired ti summon sufficent force to slap the keus

cofee is supposd to keep you awake but me not so mucj

good nihgt

zzzzzzzzzzzz

Memorandum

To: Dr. Anjali R. Sen, Esq.

From: Meredith J. Beals

Date: November 28

Subject: Noah A. Spivak (what else?)

What do you think of this very official form I found in my dad's desk drawer along with some other intriguing artifacts? I was looking for something to distract me from waiting for Noah to call me which is less intriguing than depressing but apparantly the reason he didn't until now e.g. 3:12 pm is that his mother took him to the library to get books for the infamous Micmac Project

he found one called **DIE MICMAC** which he thought was very negative until he realized it was in German hahahaha

Then he told me this other German joke

it goes like this

these guys are fighting about whose language is the most attractive

the English guy says English is best take for example Butterfly which is very descriptive butterfly flutter by

But the Spanish guy prefers Mariposa and the Italian guy says Farfalla is the most compelling

then the Franch guy objects in his Franch accent and says the word in Franch is better except i can't remember what it is

But then the German man interrupts and demands "Vots wrong vith Schmetterlink?"

Ha ha THUMP

Noah was sitting in his linen closet while he was imparting all this hilarity

He was also farting and then his mother started screaming about how he was stinking up the linens which pretty much cracked me up even though she made him get off the phone

When I reluctantly hung up Katie cross exam-
ined me in very patronizing terms and expressed
her suprize that Noah was actually calling me
and not just for homework. I did not have a quick
come back to that as I am still a bit deficient in
that regard as you know

But here's what I'm thinking

It IS true that he has not been calling me for
the homework or even to get your number which
sometimes used to happen with some boys

I THINK he is pretty much calling to talk to
me as I can't think of any other reason for him to
call unless it is to talk about you which we kind
of do alot but still the fact of the matter is that
he IS spending alot of his time with ME and that
is something I could never write before and that
is making me wonder a little bit WHY and what I
should do about it.

MJB

encl. cc. etc.

Sunday **AGAIN**

Anjali the more I think about it the more I think you are a Big Fat Liar

You said you would stick around and haunt me and now it's another week gone since you died and I have yet to receive a message

Noah says that's because I don't give you the chance and we should get a weejee board or something but as I don't have one I will do this instead I'll put my fingers on the keys and you tell me what to press

Okay here i go I'm typing this wioth my eyes shut twll me which kes to hit and then I will see the message from you

WOW! I'm actually a pretty good typist with my eyes shut. I wish they still had typinf class so I could get an easy A

But come **ON** Anjali do it! Move my fingers and leave me a message please NOW

EDAFDQ

there's not really a word there

or maybe it's a message in code

A might be you Anjali

E could be ensephilitis

Ensephilitis Die Anjali Fast Death Quick

What does that mean, Anjali? Do you mean it was so fast you couldn't give me a message?

I know how you feel--I don't know what my message would've been to you but I hate that I never got a chance to give it.

I mean it's ridiculous--I didn't even know you were sick and then you were dead from a disease I've never even heard of and can't even spell. I still don't realy know what it is or how it made you die. My mother tried to explain but I wouldn't let her and now I can tell she thinks it's because I'm afraid it will kill me too. That's not it at all but she keeps assuring me it's not catching

that is actually a big lie as it is very catching but for some reason you caught it and I didn't

it's another one of those things that doesn't really make sense. **W**HY did you catch it, Anjali, instead of me or that **BLEEPING** Wendy Mathinson? Why you??? Is it because the universe hates me???? Because it's just not fair for the universe to take you away from me, especially when I really need to ask you this question:

Do you think I should tell Noah how I feel?

I mean I do know I'm not the sort of girl someone like Noah would like. You said it yourself last September--you said I should find someone who might actually like me back to get a crush on. But here's the thing, Anjali: I'm not sure it's something you get a choice about. It might be like getting ensephilitis--you might not be able to do anything about it before it's too late. The fact of the matter is that I have always liked Noah Spivak even though I know he is Way Out of My League, just like you said.

I don't know WHY I liked him--I just did.

I just liked his sandy brown hair and his cloudy green eyes and the freakles across his nose and his braces too

I liked his gravelly gravelly voice

I like the way he gravelled "Hey Anjali, Hey Meredith," when he walked on by

in that hey there was a hint of a secret and Anjali in these past few days well I don;t know but I feel like that secret might be that there's a fragment of a fraction of a maybe of a chance that he could possibly like me a tiny bit back because the fact of the matter is that he IS spending ALOT of time with me these days

so that's what I want to know as I'm sitting here this Sunday looking out at the black blck night. What do you think, Anjali? Should I tell him how I feel?   M

November 30

wish me luck Anjali I really think I'm going to say something
to Noah this afternoon

Dear Anjali,

I don't really need to write to you for you to know what's happening here, do I? I have this feeling today more than ever that you are HERE and watching and maybe even having something to do wth the events

I am actually suspecting you're more here with me than I am with myself

maybe i am like a puppet and you are working the strings to make life the way it should be in your estimation and maybe even it's you making me say the things I'm saying since they are not actually the things I was intending to say

Or maybe you need my voice to say what your

voicelessness cannot--is that what's happening, Anjali?

Maybe it is Maybe it was you who moved my feet towards Noah after school

maybe it was you who asked him to come over for a game of Tips

maybe it was you all along because I could feel somthing in the air like electricity as we sat in the lving room with our backs against the couch our heads resting on the old sofa cushions just like you and I used to sit

I was sitting sidewise watching him, so close I could see added details I had never seen before like the freakle in the green of his left eye and as I was sitting so close the space between us felt very full of sparks--and maybe it was you moving so close to him to say to him what you didn;t ever get to say before you died because otherwise I cannot explain why the next words came out of my mouth. they were not at all the ones I'd been practicing to say and there I was saying something entirely else instead:

"Anjali always liked you, you know."

Those unintended words certainly had an immediate effect.

"What?" Noah practically shouted and that was not at all what I expected and it made me a little confused what to say next.

"I mean she REALLY liked you," I mumbled/ "She's liked you since like fifth grade. You were the first and only boy she ever liked."

Do boys cry? Noah looked like he wanted to, but then he started banging his head backward against the sofa cushion, just like the way you did the day I made you watch that movie The Savage Bees on the Creature Double Feature, when you were banging your head backwards and moaning When! Is! This! Stupid! Movie! Going! To! Be! Over! It was just like that except this time it was Noah and he was saying

"Idiot! Idiot! I KNEW I should've said something to her!!!! Meredith, do you mean if I'd asked her out LAST YEAR she would've said yes?"

(Or at least I think that's what he was saying because there was this wierd rushing in my ears and I couldn't really hear but over the rushing I thought I heard him saying "idiot idiot idiot--I **KNEW** I should've said something to her before" over and over again so I tried to comfort him awkwardly by putting my arm around his shoulder which is when my mother opened the door to the living room and asked to speak to me for a moment in private

she then informed me she's not so comfortable with me being alone with boys with the door shut which made me slightly hysterical

after that Noah went home, still looking like he might want to cry because of the ridiculous and total unfairness of discovering you both liked each other but finding out only after you **DIED**

I mean when you think of it is pretty tragical I mean him turning out to like you all along and you not knowing that and him not knowing that you had just started liking him too, ~~and me b~~

well anyway it's pretty cruddy

But here's what I'm thinking, Anjali: don't you feel a LITTLE bit lucky, for all that you're dead? I mean, **NOAH SPIVAK!!!!** Just like 3 months ago you were deciding you liked him, and now here he is saying he likes you back so if I was you I'd be jumping up and down and coming back to life right now I really would so help me god--if Noah Spivak liked ME like that there is **NO WAY** I'd let myself be dead.

m

November 31

Dear Anjali,

Here's a funny thing--if Noah was writing this
letter he'd probably say it was a **GREAT** day

he came bouncing up to me before English and
he was beaming all over like the universe had
just given him a birthday present

I cannot exactly comprehend his contentment
given that the universe also just took away his
birthday present before he even got it e.g. by kill-
ing you but he seems to think that just knowing
you liked him is enough he cannot shut up about
it actually

all he wants me to repeat is when you started

liking him and all these details until I'm like I **DON'T KNOW ALREADY ASK ANJALI** but of course he **CAN'T** because **YOU'RE DEAD** and all he can do is come over to my house and look at the old pictures and have me resurrect you for him.

i don't know

usually talking about you makes me feel closer to you but this time it just made me feel b

l

a

h

Maybe it's because it's so ridiculous and depressing that you guys never even really met.

i don't know Anjali

sometimes I think the universe has a mean streak a billion light years wide.

Apparantly it changed months while I wasn't paying attention. Now it's my birthday in like two days but I am not feeling very festive given that my best friend is **DEAD** and everything else is messed up

I felt so down this morning I could barely get out of bed so my mother let me take a Mental Health Day^{TM} from school as long as I went to see Dartin in the afternoon.

I don't know why she's wasting her money!!!!! It's such a colossal waste of time!!!!!! Here is an example:

Him: Well Meredith, how have you been feeling this week?

Me: Okay, I guess. <-- NOTE: a lie.

Him: Trouble sleeping?

Me: No.

(You can tell this is word-for-word verbatim because you can't make up brilliant sparky dialog like this even with a degree in Dialogology^{TM}).

Him: I see your birthday is coming up on Friday. Will that be strange to have without your friend Anjali?

Me: **ARE** YOU **KIDDING** ME???? **EVER**Y day is strange without my friend Anjali!!!!!! You can't IM**AGINE** how stupid my life is without her.

That moron is totally overpaid let me tell you instead they should pay ME to suffer through that miserable hour of him thinking he understands me. I tell you Anjali the only thing worse than not being understood is when people think they Understand You^{TM} and don't. It is very obvious this moron does not understand Jack Squat about me. Here is an example of the Squat he comes up with. According to him the reason you were so important to me is that you were my MIRROR which let me see myself and know I was alright. I told him he was wrong that if you were a MIRROR you just showed me how spazzy and ugly I am in comparison to you and in point of fact the reason you were so important to me was the simple fact that you were MY **BEST FRIEND** but he was too enamored of his own stupid overpriced theories to listen. He kept rapsodizing about how it matters that you CHOSE ME which of course matters **ALOT** but for the fact that you are **DEAD** and the fact that no one is choosing me NOW and that's the point and that's why Dartin is an idiot.

Later i found this pamphlet he must've given my mother to explain what I am Going Through. It is by this lady scientist who says there are 5 stages of grief: Denial (not just a river in Egypt); Anger (why did this happen to me????); Bargaining (if you make this not true I'll never be mean to Katie again); Depression (blah...); and Acceptance ("I think I'll be okay.")

Here is my progression:

Denial: I am not ever going to feel better.

Anger: Stop telling me I'm going to feel better!

Bargaining: I won't kill you if you stop telling me I'll feel better.

Depression: (Okay, this one is accurate. I will admit that I am feeling a little depressed.)

Acceptance: I guess I really am going to feel depressed forever

Ha ha ha hah blah

Here are some more stages of grief: brush teeth. Pajamas. Scowl at Katie. Good night.

12/3 = 4

(in math class)

Today is a cruddy day.

It's pouring rain outside and everyone's in a bad mood and the whole school is filled with the nasty choking smell of wet wool

Dr. Carr gave us a pop quiz in Civics and I had not in point of fact done the reading

then at lunch that wierd kid Arnold had a fit at the cash register like he did last year

there was this whole traffic jam because no one could get by him

I will say it again, Anjali: that space was designed by a moron.

Anyway they had to give everyone their lunches for free just to get them through the line because no one could get him to move or stop crying

So now I have 2 bucks of my very own thanks to Arnold

it's wierd

No one knows why he was crying.

I don't know why either but I kind of know how he feels.

WHAT'S WRONG WITH ME, ANJALI!?!?!?!?!?!?!?!?!?!?!?!?

After school Noah came up to me and asked if he could come over to play leper poker which is where you throw down your hand when you fold but I was so blah apparantly he got bored and went home at 4:11 even though he'd previously said he could stay until dinner

after he left I couldn't help it and called him twice but he hasn't called back, not even once. Now instead of doing my homework I've been sitting here at my desk looking up at the ugly water stain on the cieling

you and I used to argue about whether it

looked more like a horse or foot but frankly I just don't care anymore--it just looks brown and ugly.

I really don't know what's wrong with me.

Katie just came in here and asked me what was up with my boyfriend

I tried to explain to her that Noah Spivak is in no way my boyfriend

then she explained that the reason he is not my boyfriend and why no boys are ever my boyfriend is because I am in fact too moody and depressive.

She says boys are very shallow and not at all interested in sorrow and if I want them to like me I should always be U^P happy tra la la la la

I bet she's right but I cannot make myself all CHIPPER and UPBEAT these days

I would like to be all sunshine and light and everything but in case you have not noticed MY BEST FRIEND IS DEAD which makes it a little overcast.

somedays instead of sunshine and light all I

can see is creeping black muck oozing out of the
desks and doors and windows drowning me

which is why that even if I am driving Noah
away by being so

                    d

                         o

                              w

                                   n

I don't think I have alot of choice in the matter

~~I'll tell you what's worse than finding half a worm in
you're apple, Anjali. It's finding out that the boy you like is
in love with your b~~

                                   (after dinner)

Noah still hasn't called. I guess I shouldn't be
suprized--I guess I should've been suprized instead

that he did hang out with me all of those days last week. I mean it's obvious I'm not the sort of person someone like Noah Spivak would like. That's what we always said, and I know it's true. I'm not like you Anjali--you were beautiful and funny and mostly not moody and I bet you could've been one of the popular kids if you hadn't been saddled with me I mean I know Wendy Mathinson only hated you because she thought you might have my nerd germs on you but otherwise I think she wouldn't have objected to you joining the Evil Oasis

so for all those reasons it does not suprize me really that Noah likes you and not me.

I should've known it all alone I mean all along

what should've made me wonder instead is why YOU were willing to have my nerd germs on you

sometimes this fall I worried that you wouldn't forever and in those times I felt I really need to know why you put up with me when I'm so ugly and spazzy. I asked you that, remember? But instead of answering, you said,

"Maybe I WON'T be friends with you anymore, if you go around fishing for compliments like that."

I hadn't thought I was fishing

or maybe I WAS fishing because I did need to know that you like m.

And the thing is I STILL nd to know, Anjali, for all that YOUR DAD

I man dad

what the hck????

???

did I just los th lttr that gos btwn d and f?????

Com on--giv it back!!!!!! I us that lttr alot.

Anjali--ar you snding m a mssag that I shouldn't b sitting around hr sulking?

Ha ha Anjali

You always had a funny sns of humor.

December 4th

ironically 12:04 in the A.M.

Blah.

I just looked at the clock

it's my birthday now and not only is my best friend DEAD but the e on my typewriter is broken.

It doesn't FEEL like my birthday.

I think I have never felt so unfestive in all my life

morning

God I miss my typewriter

Now it's my birthday and I'm stuck going to school. There should be a lawsuit against it but my mother says that as I have already availed myself of one Mental Health™ day this week I have to go. Then she asked me if I wanted to have a birthday party this weekend. ¿¿¿¿????

That is doubly dumb as you'd think she'd remember my best friend just DIED plus as I told her birthday parties are for babies.

At least I <u>think</u> they're for babies, but I could be wrong. I mean I haven't been invited to a party for a long time but that may just be me. What do you think, Anjali? Is everyone but me going to Halloween parties and Thanksgiving parties and Martin Luther King Day parties all the time?

Actually I take that question back—I don't really want to know. Sometimes it's better to be in the dark.

Back home now—I should've skipped the middle man and played hookey. I knew it was going to be a cruddy day as soon as I walked in the door. All those stupid kids were sitting in the Evil Oasis and laughing at me when I tripped over someone's backpack they probably left there on purpose.

I will not keep you in suspense: the day did not get better, which leads me to a question: are you still a year older if your birthday is totally cruddy? Because it kind of feels like a rip-off. Somebody better give me "American Beauty" as a present at my birthday dinner tonight—that's all I have to say about it

Can you believe it, Anjali?

A year ago I got to go to the indoor water park for my birthday with you and without Katie and I got garnet earrings from my grandmother on top of the usual swag

This year you are DEAD and my grandmother sent me NOTHING except a subscription to National Geographic Magazine which she won for free doing on-line surveys because she is on a fixed income and the market is down and of course I understand, don't I, dear?

Sure thing

To make it up to me my mother announced we would have a Fancy Girl's Night Out™ to celebrate. That would have been some consolation but for the fact that her idea of an exquisite locale was the lousy Château Nouvelle

I don't know if you ever went but the Château Nouvelle is this very cruddy restaurant which pretends to be fancy

I used to be tricked because of it's golf I mean gold wall-paper which is alternately shiny and velvet

Also they bring the pizza to you on a tall stand so that

you can't see anyone across the table which is not so bad when you are out with Katie who is trying to look very grown up with her hair all teased and verticle and a new dress that's so tight I'm amazed my mother let her out of the house

As I said I used to think the Châtéaii Nouvelle was elegant but now I know the truth it is not so much fancy as fakey and destined for disaster

The restaurant was very full and we could not get seated in the room with the gold wallpaper nor the room with the red wallpaper neither (I guess you can understand that since three's a crowd you know)

You will notice from my account that my father did not choose to come to this celebratory event

he apparantly felt that being stuck by snow in the Cleveland airport was more intriguing than going to dinner with his TEENAGE daughter for her thirteenth birthday.

In the end they found a corner of a table for us in the blue room

In case you do not know, the blue room is in the Châtéaii Nouvelle BASEMENT it does not have velvet wallpaper at all

it's walls are shiny metallic swirly blue

There are framed Star Wars posters on the shiny metallic swirly blue wallpaper which are very familiar as they are the exact same ones we have in our bathroom which my mother bought when she was 9 years old.

Let me tell you it does not feel like your birthday is very special when you are eating in a bathroom designed by your 9 year old mother

Jezum Crow!

The waiter brought Katie a wineglass when he brought my mother's

Katie flirted with him in the most disgusting fashion which made me want to barf or maybe that was the fault of the undercooked yet greasy pizza

I think my mother knew I was Not Happy because she kept asking me if I wanted the eggplant parmagan instead

she kept calling it "THE PARM"

"Are you <u>sure</u> you don't want THE PARM?" she asked. "I know you love THE PARM." "Maybe we should've ordered THE PARM."

Here's the thing of it: THE PARM is not going to bring my best friend back to life nor make Noah want to hang out with me neither. What might make me feel better is to have my mother stop giving nicknames to food!!!

then the perky waiters brought out a cake with a candle in it and sang happy birthday

They sang it to Katie

She didn't tell them not to she probably wanted them to think she was turning 35

Then I dropped frosting down my shirt and when I tried to clean it up Katie squealed that I was trying to stuff my bra

I realized later I should've told her I'd rather have an empty bra than an empty brain but I am still very bad at that comeback thing.

Then my mother brought out the presents

For a moment I thought I was going to get all the great stuff I told her I needed

I could even see my "American Beauty" CD there all wrapped up and tied with ribbons except when I tore off the paper it was a bleeping DESK CALANDER with these cats in sneakers on it. What am I going to do with a DESK

CALANDER I ask you????? Write down how many days it has been since you DIED? It's not like I am in need of recording my many social engagements LORD

Also I got 3 books which in theory I like but in practice always feel like a letdown ditto clothes

THINGS just seem more like presents like the plastic earrings you gave me with that card that said IT'S THE THOUGHT THAT COUNTS.

I can totally tell no one thought about my presents this year because they were so exceptionally dumb especially the one from Katie who gave me a leather diary and a fountain pen (??????). Maybe she thought it was my 30th birthday and not my 13th she does get confused sometimes. It is somewhat of a tragedy that she was born without a BRAIN

Or maybe she wants me to stay committed to my typerwriter-less state so I am not click clack clacking like little needles to her head

hahahahahahaha wish again Katie I am a WRITER an AUTHOR just like our grandmother says (in case you were wondering Katie is the BEAUTY and our cousin Whitney is HER OWN PERSON ha ha). Once my typerwriter is back

I will type all day and all night spewing my brilliant thoughts into the ether and you can put that in the bank and write a check on it

or better yet take it out and buy me a GOOD PRESENT FOR A CHANGE!!!

P.S. It's 11:59. It's such a lousy feeling, late on the night of your birthday, knowing you won't have a chance to have a non-cruddy birthday for a whole nother year.

December 5ive

Feeling particularly mopey this morning for a change looking at my new BOOKS and my PEN and my DESK CALANDER. Why would my family think THIS was the landfill I wanted? It's like they've been living with me for the past 13 years and they don't know me at all.

I guess I shouldn't be suprized—sometimes I think you were the only one who ever knew me. There are times these days when I feel totally INVISIBLE or maybe INSCRUTIBLE but when I was with you I always felt both visible and scrutible

Now the only times I feel visible are times when invisibility would come in handy but instead I find myself s w e l L I N G up like a big pimply Thanksgiving Macy's Day parade and everyone's pointing and laughing not so much with me as at me especially Wendy god I hate her what gives her permission to hate me

so much????? It's enough to make me want to D-I-E
actually knowing it might be that no one will ever see
me again.

I dunno. I've been sitting here and thinking about what
your dad once said about colors. "What if the color you see
as red is what I see as blue?" he asked. "What if when I talk
about a "red" apple I'm actually seeing the color you call
"blue," even though I think that color is called "red"? How
would you ever know I don't see what you see?"

And really maybe that's what it's like. Maybe you and
me recognized each other as blue-seeing apples and that's
why we were always friends. And maybe it was just us—
maybe no one else will ever be able to see what we saw. Or
maybe that's not what I mean. Sometimes I sit here writing
and stuff comes out and I don't know if it's really DEEP
or really STUPID

sometimes I think there's a fine line between DEEP and
STUPID, actually

meredeath

I'm in a little less bad of a mood right now

    that is in part because the phone just rang

    for once it was not for Katie

    it was FOR ME

    Anyway it was NOAH, calling to wonder how I was on account of our not talking so much at the end of last week. He was much nicer than he has been for the past few days especially after he found out it has been my birthday. He comiserated with me over the sack of sewage I got instead of birthday presents and said he should come over and whup me in a birthday game of Tips which is an intriguing idea. Unfortunately he couldn't because my dad was on the way back from Cleveland to belatedly becelebrate my bebirthday

    Then my dad came in and pretended not to recognize me as I am now a teeanger and all. He promised to take me anywhere I wanted for dinner so we are going to go to the Bombay Club even though Katie hates that kind of thing

He also gave me my present which was not so much the iPod I asked for but instead (drum beat) an AM/FM CLOCK RADIO!!!!!!!!!!!! (sounds of excited celebration)

(that was sarcastic, in case you didn't get it)

I should not be so critical of this stereophonic object actually

it may not be all slick and loaded with "American Beauty" like I asked but it does have "Frequency Modulation" and "Amplitude Modulation" as well (nothing but the finest in modern technology for my dad)

I have a Hopeful Theory™

perhaps if I tuuuunnnee my radio to the right station using the Frequency Modulator your voice will come out of the statatatic (good thing I got a radio not a fish because you can't tuna fish)

!!!!! !!!!!!!!! !!!!!!!!!!!!!!!!!!!!!!!!!!!!!!!!!!!!!!!

and holy moly! !!!!

Just as I'm tuning the radio it's playing "Ripple" by the Greatful Dead!!!!!!!!!!!

Is that you sending me a message? Cause I swear it's like you're SINGING TO ME THROUGH THE RADIO

♪ "would you hear my voice come through the music" ♫

I do! I do! I hear you, Anjali!

♫ "reach out your hand if your cup be empty" ♪
(that's obviously me)
♪ "if your cup is full may it be again" ♪
(???? I don't actually get this.)

la la la la la ←that's what you're singing now
no truer words were ever spoken

it's good to hear your voice, Anjali.
I've been really missing you.

Sunday

I hate Sundays!!! It's partially because you died on a Sunday and now for all of the Sundays for the rest of my life I will be thinking about your dying but that's not the only reason—I've always hated them. There's just something about the sun going down on a Sunday evening that always makes me feel a little scared, like I want to be home and know everything's going to be okay. It's much worse now. Sometimes it feels like a door opened after you died, a door into the blackness, and it hasn't quite shut since. That makes everything much scarier. It's just so dark outside and cold and that makes me think of wherever you are if there's no heaven and you're just floating in space in the frozen darkness. I hate that thought! Whenever I think it I try really hard to unthink it quick but then there are times like tonight when my dad made me go to the garage for mousetraps and it was so dark and cold I felt like death's fingers were going to reach out and drag me through that hole—

I hate the night and the dark and December.

Sometimes I think December is the Sunday Night of the year.

God I feel so alone!!!!! Every time another week passes it makes me feel worse, like it's even more impossible to rescue you

I mean, I kind of know I never could've saved you once you were dead but the further I get away from that moment the more impossible it feels. I just keep thinking about one of those movies on the Creature Double Feature where the monster is coming and someone's falling behind and their hand slips out of your grasp and then you're running and running to save yourself but you keep looking back at the trapped person but with every footstep it's harder to go back and then you see the monster or the tidal wave or whatever and the people get this stricken look like they know they can never go back now and save their friends and they cover their faces and the music swells

that's what it's like, like as the weeks go on it's more and more impossible to go back and save you.

Now all I can do is write to you EVERY DAY to keep you here with me But how am I going to make it, Anjali???????

sometimes I think I can do it, but other days I know there's no way I can.

m

Off to school!

I'm feeling a little more cherry this AM

I didn't tell you but Noah called last night and said he had something to give me at school

That is very intriguing.

What do you think it is?

later (in math)

Here's the thing, Anjali: I really need you to be alive right now because I need to know what to do.

The something Noah gave me is a card, a birthday card, like the kind he'd had to of bought with real money in a real store. I have in fact recieved cards before so that is not the problem—the trouble is what it says on the front:

~~I just want you to know how I feel~~

I haven't opened it yet because for some reason I am feeling very worried or maybe even what I'm feeling is dread even though I don't know why. I mean I'm not sure what the card could say that would upset me. I mean if it turns out he HATES me he wouldn't go and spend $3.75 to tell me that, right??? On the other hand I do not think they make cards that say "I kind of liked spending time with you before I discovered you are a bit of a downer" so I'm not sure what Noah could want to be telling me with that card

I mean what seems most likely is that he is saying ~~he likes m~~

but obviously that's not it because I mean I know he likes YOU

I mean if you were still alive he'd probably be your BOYFRIEND if you in fact figured out that you both like each other so that can't be what the card says but still

~~I mean, maybe, since you are d~~

I guess I have to open it

I feel fine, thanks. How are you?

at lunch

ANJALI!!!!!!!!!!!!!!!!

Was that card supposed to be nice or mean????? Was
it making fun of me, or was it supposed to be a funny joke
hahaha to cheer me up? I really can't tell because really
it's only funny if I thought that he was going to say something else

Oh God GOD that means that he would have to think
that I was going to think that it was going to say that he li
you don't think he thought that I thought that, do you?
I didn't think that, really I didn't!!!!!!!!!!!!!!!
did ~~he know what I was trying to say that day when I told~~
~~him you liked~~ him
    is he making fun of me???????

Look Anjali I want to make sure you understand something

I know Noah liked you and not me

I know if you weren't dead he'd be your boyfriend and I would never try to take him away (not that I could)

I know I'm not the sort of girl he would ever go out with I KNOW THAT of course I do I've heard it all my life even before you pointed it out to me

I mean even my own MOTHER knows I'm not the sort of girl boys like.

She's always saying I have an inner beauty

I guess she means that all I have to look forward to in life is an inner boyfriend.

w.

(that's an m with it's legs in the air because I just give up)

WHY DID HE DO THAT TO ME??????

December 8th

ANJALI!!!! HOW AM I SUPPOSED TO KNOW IF NOAH IS NICE OR A JERK????

All I can do is avoid him.

This morning I snuck in the side door so I didn't have to see him hanging out with the snot brigade. And why WOULD he hang out with them, unless he's the sort of person who would send me that card to make fun of me? The fact is that he is a big mystery and maybe a dangerous one—I'm not sure I should trust him. I'm not sure if I should ever trust anyone, actually (except you, I mean.)

back at home sitting on my bed staring at the horse-shaped stain on the cieling. I just realized what day it is: it's one month after you died. All last week I was planning to suprize you today by going and visiting your grave so you could see it but then I was so busy sneaking out of school early that I forgot. But now that I'm thinking about it I guess you probably already know what your grave looks like. I mean, why am I assuming you're always hanging around here with me, so that you need me to bring you places? For all I know you're spending your days hanging out with Noah and Wendy Mathinson.

December 9
11:52 am in the almost afternoon

I just found this note stuck in my locker

MEREDITH. GET SICK DURING SIXTH PERIOD.

What does it mean? Do you think you should follow locker orders you get like that? I'm so BLEEPING confused.

WHY AREN'T YOU HERE TO HELP ME, ANJALI????
Where ARE you??????
I NEED you to tell me what to do
it's fifth period now

LATER. Hey Anjali—Can you read this if I write it on a computer? I have to use my father's to write a piece of fiction for Pritchard. What do you think of this?

Scene: Confused GIRL thinks that maybe she is getting sick during sixth period. She moans her way to the nurse. The school corridors are empty and damp. The footsteps echo like a lonely cry. THE NURSE says to go in quietly because another student is there resting. THE GRIL opens the door to the back room, and sees THE BOY lying on the hard purple cot. He opens one eye and winks. THE GIRL isn't sure how to act. THE NURSE motions for THE GIRL to lie down. THE GIRL doesn't want to because it's way too wierd to lie down in front of THE BOY. THE GIRL sits.)

THE NURSE: I'll go get you a glass of water.

(THE BOY waits for tHE NURSE to leave.)

THE BOY (*A little mad*): Why are you avoiding me, Meredith? What's going on? Are you mad at me or something?

(*THE GIRL is even more confused. She lies down and looks at the cieling so she doesn't have to look at THE BOY. She can't tell him why she's been avoiding him. If she tells him she thinks that he was making fun of her by teasing that he LIKES HER that's the same as admitting that she ever thought for a moment that it was possible that he could LIKE HER. That is just too embarasing for words. THE GIRL says nothing.*)

THE GIRL:

(*THE BOY rubs his nose angrily*).

THE BOY: If you're mad at me you should at least tell me what I did!

THE GIRL: (*without meaning to, really. It was like I couldn't stop myself, it just blurted out.*) Were you making fun of me?

THE BOY: WHAT?????

THE GIRL: Were you making fun of me with that card???

THE BOY (*Throwing up his hands*): God, Wendy was right! You're crazy.

THE GIRL: See, that's what I mean! I bet you're always making fun of me with Wendy Mathinson!! But I don't care because she's a DRIED PIECE OF SNOT and she always laughs at me and I don't know how you can be friends with her unless you're a snot too!

THE BOY: What are you talking about??? Are you mental or something?

THE GIRL: FQBRDEGAFRAG![1]

THE BOY: You think you're so smart, but you don't know me at all.

And THE BOY, miraculously cured, stalks out of the nurse's office, and THE GIRL, miraculously sick, lies down until THE NURSE calls her mother and says she better come pick THE GIRL up.

THE END

---

[1] I don't know what she was saying either.

Meredith Beals

Mrs. Pritchard

English

December 10

My Canteen and I

The hot sand burned my throat and my eyes glazed over as I reached for my canteen that should've held water. It did not. It was as dry as my mouth, dry as the sand that surrounded us for miles. We were alone, my canteen and I, in the middle of the desert, with the winds blowing over us, blowing the sand over the desert like a mist, hiding the dusty view from us like a veil.

The mist parted, displaying an every day street, one I have walked down so many times before. In my pocket there was money, quarters and nickels and dimes that would buy a drink to quench my unquenchable thirst.

The Coke came tumbling out of the machine,

and I grabbed it, tearing off the top—but nothing came out of it.

I opened my eyes, I was just staring at the empty canteen. I was still surrounded by sand. The stones, not coins, which I clutched in my hand were dark with my sweat. I dropped the empty canteen down on the sand. It made the faintest thud, but this sounded like that last breath a dying animal takes.

I could see the tracks my camel had made, running off with my food and water, back to the place he called home.

My home was not this dry desert, not this place of howling winds and endless smell of sand and hot. Not at all.

If I just kept walking I would soon come to my house. I rose to my feet, picking up the canteen and cradling it in my arms. In my arms I was carrying some bread that I had trotted down to the store to get. I mounted the stairs.

My mother answers the door. I walk after her

into the kitchen. She pours me some water. She questions me about the desert—I am just back. I am very thirsty from my walk and reach for the water. I bring my hand to my mouth.

I spit out sand, and more sand, and fall to my knees. Next to me was the canteen, no mother, no home, no water. We are alone in the desert. We are alone, my canteen and I, in the lonely desert, surrounded by sand and howling winds. We are alone, with no Coke machine to quench our thirst. We are alone, my canteen and I, with no mother to hand us water. We are alone, my canteen and I, alone.

Very imaginative, Meredith!
But how can you quench
unquenchable thirst?
That's an oxymoron,
don't you agree?

A/A—

HEY MEREDITH

I LIKED YOUR STORY

I REALLY MEAN IT. I **REALLY** LIKED
YOUR STORY.

IT'S ABOUT ANJALI, ISN'T IT?

NO It's not about Anjali. It's just a story. I just wrote it
because I didn't have anything else to write about.

OH. I THOUGHT IT WAS ABOUT LOSING
ANJALI AND BEING ALONE.

Well it wasn't.

OR MAYBE IT WAS THAT YOU THOUGHT YOU
FOUND SOMEONE TO BE FRIENDS WITH AFTER
HER AND THEN YOU THOUGHT HE WAS A JERK.

It's just a story. Just a stupid story.

WELL ANYWAY. WILL YOU MEET ME BY THE ROCK
AFTER SCHOOL? I REALLY NEED TO TALK TO YOU.

Anjali for the love of Mike would you please not be dead? For the first time since you I died I want you to be alive not because then I wouldn't be miserable but because we would've all been actually HAPPY together. I had such a GOOD DAY!!! And again with the exclamation points!!! And three times three!!! !!! !!!

It was BLEEPING cold when I got to the rock. Noah was all jumping up and down when I got there and whacking at his nose with these big Andean mittens he wears.

"My nose feels funny," he was complaining.

"That's just your boogers freezing," I informed him.

"I didn't know girls talked about boogers," he commented, and that was the wierd part, because suddenly we didn't need to talk about the card and the nurse's office or anything—we were just making booger jokes together. And then he said "Do you want to get cofee?"

"No," I said. "I had another idea—but it involves a bus and the subway and another bus and is kind of a big deal."

"What is it?" he asked me with curious suspicion.

"I want to go visit Anjali's grave."

"How do you know I was thinking that?????? " he shouted, 200 question marks.

I don't know why but just waiting for the bus was totally fun when it was with Noah Spivak. We made all these dumb jokes which I would tell you about except that when I tried them out on Katie she said they were very sophmoronic so I guess you just kind of had to be there. We were all giddy and giggly like you and I used to get but then when we got on the bus I suddenly had this really wierd idea. There was this guy who came running up just as the bus was pulling away, bags bouncing, hat falling off, and the driver didn't stop for him at all. Noah and I watched from the back window and there was that frustrated and angry person watching us pull away until he got smaller and smaller in a puff of exhaust. Then he was gone but I realized there's a place where HE was still standing there and WE were the ones getting smaller and

smaller in a puff of exhaust, getting so small that we disap-
peared. And then this was the wierd thought: what if that's
the way it is with you? Maybe you're still somewhere living on
in some way and it's all of us who are getting smaller and
smaller to you. That is a very wierd idea and I'm not sure I
like it but that's what I was thinking when I suddenly noticed
we hadn't said anything in a long time and then I saw that
Noah was kind of staring at me intently and we both got kind
of embarased and then he said,

"What's that necklace you're wearing?"

So I told him about the night on the Ferris wheel (but not
the part where you and I were talking about whether you'd
leave me in a puff of exhaust if it turned out Noah liked
you) and then he said, "I think that necklace is turning your
neck green."

That's when I told him about how I am going to wear it
FOREVER irrespective of the neck gangreen and how I was
going to write to you EVERY DAY so you could know what I was
thinking, and he said, "Why do you need to WRITE to her? Why
can't she just HEAR things you say?" And he waved to you,
like people do when they suddenly realize they're on TV.

It hadn't really occured to me before that you might be able to HEAR me—it just seems more logical to me that you can read what I'm writing. Maybe it's because I just FEEL you're closer when I write to you. I really do. I mean, I'm just sitting here now and it's like I can FEEL you looking at the pen as it moves across the page w a i t i n g for me to get to what you want to hear (I'm teasing you now) w a t c h i n g each slow lagubrious letter (that's my new word which I don't really know the meaning of) w i s h i n g I would hurry up and get to the point—

Here's a point: most other people apparantly think the deceased mostly hang out around their graves. The cematary is full of things people leave for their dead friends. Alot of flowers. Flags. A can of Moxie soda (?????). There's this one grave that's surrounded by all sorts of stuffed animals, just like people left near the pond when Kristi Lawrence drownded that winter, all those little bears in plastic bags so they wouldn't rot in the rain.

This little girl whose grave was all covered with bears was only 5 years old when she died, but she's older than we are now, or at least she would've been, except for the fact of

being dead. It's very confusing. How old is she, for all intensive purposes? Five? Seventeen? When her parents pass her birthday, do they think, here it is again, Sandy's 5th birthday? Or do they think she's growing up, somewhere? What will happen when they see her again? Will they recognize her? And what does it mean to see her again? I mean, even if she's the same, they won't be. And if people stay the age they are when they die forever that is not exactly fair to the old people—though I guess they were lucky that they lived so long in the first place, when other people died when they were 13. Actually, I don't want to think about that. It kind of makes me kind of queasy

Here's something morbid: I like the graveyard. I like the statues and the sad little lambs on the graves that say "baby" and the stone dogs standing guard over masters who are never going to go for walks again. There are famous people who Did Things in Life and have big monuments and then there all these stones with no names at all, stones that just say "Father" or "Mother" or "Daughter" on them. Noah said that was kind of depressing because the people were such Losers they didn't even have their names anymore but that's

not how I see it. It's true you don't know anything about those people but you do know someone loved them and that might actually tell you alot.

One of the famous buried people there is this lady Mary Baker Eddie

I don't know if anyone loved her but Noah tells me she has a telephone in her grave so she can call people if she turns out to suddenly be alive again

we are going to write a story about it because it turns out that Noah is something of a secret writer

in our story Mary Baker Eddie wakes up and calls and calls but everyone thinks it's a crank

we are going to call it "Wrong Number" hahahaha

We decided to write some other stories and set them in the graveyard as it is an intriguing locale

there's this tall romantic tower which we have climbed

there are all these frozen ponds and these "one way" signs which are very amusing in a graveyard ha ahahahahah (it's funny because it's true)

We planned out the scenes in another story we might write by acting them out racing through the stones and hiding in the bushes. That sounds like playing pretend except that we of course are too old for that now instead we are WRITERS which is a very mature profession if you don't know. On the other hand it must've looked a little bit like playing because this man came out and said we had to stop being disrespectful to the dead. After he left we decided that in actuality we were being very extra respectful to the dead because we were providing entertainment for you. I hope you were entertained because I sprained my ankle in the middle of all that vigorous writing and it stills huuuurrrts

Noah said he felt very close to you in that graveyard but I have to say I don't

I think I feel the same close to you all the time though sometimes I worry that maybe I'm fooling myself

or maybe it's like that time I was so upset about Katie and I was lying on your bed with my head in the pillow and bemoaning about it for like an hour and it turned out you weren't even listening at all but just reading a comic book the whole time. PUT DOWN THE COMIC BOOK ANJALI SO I CAN TELL YOU ABOUT NOAH

it was so fun getting lost there

we worried for a while that not only would we not find your grave but we might never find the way out again and have to cannibalize the visitors ha ha

that was when we found the tower and climbed up to orient ourselves

it was wierd but when we got to the top we could see that we had been completely backwards in our understanding.

From up there everything was all spread out like a map, which made me realize you sometimes need 3 dimensions to make sense of 2.

From up in that dimension we could see everything: the gate, the windy road, the pond, and the grove where the man had said your grave was. Then we both remembered why we were there (not that we had really forgotten) and we climbed somberly down and made our way through the serene weeping trees to the place where you are buried.

We stood there a long time on top of your grave. It was actually kind of awful, thinking of you there under the ground. I got all misty then and my nose burned despite the cold and when I looked over I saw Noah was choking up a bit too and that made me feel very sorry for him, because he lost you before he even ever found you, while at least I got all those 9 years being your best friend, and that was something. But then he squatted down and put a little pebble on the metal marker where your gravestone will be when they get around to it.

"What did you do that for?" I asked him.

"I don't know," he said. "That's what my mother does, when she goes to visit my grandfather." So I did too.

We didn't really talk after that. First I sat down, and then he did, and we sat there looking at those pebbles on the marker and kind of leaning up against each other. We didn't need to talk. We sat there without talking for a long time, each thinking about you, and it might've been the best conversation we ever had.

December 11

After school, sitting in my room. And why am I not off with your boyfriend Noah Abram Spivak you may well ask? Well that is because of something I didn't tell you last night because my fingers were all cramping up and I was tired of writing. It turns out that my parents are sadly not so cool with me going into the city after all, especially when I miss the bus coming back and am an hour and a half late for dinner instead of just a half an hour late as I had intended.

They were very testy about it and reminded me that I could've called which was technically possible but for the difficulty that I had previously bought cofee with my emergency quarters

Now instead of them buying me a cellphone which is the obvious solution I am grounded which is very much of a bummer. That's why I'm just here writing away with my FoUnTaIn PeN given to me by my sister KaTiE who is being uncharacteristically nice to me these days. (Getting grounded for hanging out with a boy has apparently raised me in her estimation)

I am also waiting for a certain person whose name is kavipS haoN in Hebrew to call me as he said he would

it was so funny in English today! Whenever I turned around he was looking at me and when he turned around I was looking at him and then we started trying to look at each other without being caught which was very amusing but in the end led to me cracking up and getting my desk moved

PHONE!

Okay, that was bleepin' 'ILARIOUS. I was talking to Noah (about you, always about you, don't worry) when I decided to make toast in the new toaster oven. I had this brilliant idea that it might be better to butter it first which actually wasn't so brilliant as evidenced by the fact that the toaster oven caught on actual fire

Noah was saying something funny and I didn't want to interrupt him so I unplugged the toaster and threw it out the back door into the snow to extinguish it

I forgot to get it later so it was still there when my mother
came home and questioned me quizzically about it

ha hahahahah

Noah says it is better to fry toast in butter he will show
me when we're allowed to hang out again

whoa

that was a little wierd

usually when I say "we" I mean me'n'you, not me'n'Noah

I am not excluding you though Anjali of course I am
assuming that you are coming along—you know I want you
there, don't you?

merrydith!

P.S. Noah wants my email adress. I don't want to give him the one
I use to write to my grandmother with because headchog@bpm.com
does not really represent me any longer since a) I learned how to
spell and b) I got out of my hedgehog phase. Getting a new one
seems very stressful though—it's kind of like getting a tattoo.
I mean meredithbeals@ seems very lame but I am not really the
sort of person who can pull off coolgurrl197 or something like that

what about flatchested@a32.com

I wish I could use symbols. Then I could just cut to the chase and be @@.com

Why do you think Noah wants me to have an email account, anyway????

P.P.S. Guess what Pritchard told me today? It's not P.S.S. actually but P.P.S. instead. Apparantly it stands for post (after) scriptum (written) and although I'm not sure why it can't be post (after) scriptum (written) scriptum (written) it is apparantly supposed to be post (after) post (after) scriptum (written). Actually I think it would make more sense to write scriptum (written) post (after) post (after) scriptum (written), but apparantly that is not the rule.

P.P.P.S. Apparantly the rule is also that you are not supposed to write post scriptums in English papers either. So there you go. Live and learn. Or I guess in your case you can die and learn, too.

P.P.P.P.S. That didn't offend you, did it, Anjali?

HI HI HI

This is MJB back on ~~th~~ my bust-up writing apparatus

though I am without an "E" it can still do fun things ~~lik~~ such as this:

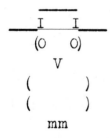

that is a bird sporting a jaunty hat

or this

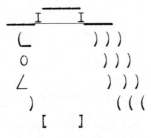

that is a similarily hat-sporting man

also I could talk with you if I pay good mind to what words I am choosing in this way:

My own Anjali

A short communication for I must study for a big quiz in that class in which I study books, that class taught by Miss Pritchard. It is ~~v~~ muy cruddy that this word-putting-down apparatus is still non-functioning. Told my ~~fath~~ dad that I must fix said apparatus but said dad informs ~~m~~ yours truly that it is too costly to fix this thing and that his digital 1 works good for writing. Said dad also said that in this hour I am thinking of words with only As and Is and Os and Us and occasional WHYs I could do all my school work and also wash all our family's food apparati. Perhaps said dad is right. Good night.

Mrdith

Sunday, December 13

Aaaaaaaahhh Friday the 13th comes on a Sunday this month
    I tell you Anjali I cannot wait for school tomorrow
    I never thought I'd write that
    phone restriction does that to a person
    it's sad when the most exciting thing you can imagine is
passing notes in English class
    do you think we will?

m

December 14

Hey Anjali!!!

remember all those times I wanted to watch the Creature
Double Feature and you said all those old creepy movies with
Lon Chaney or Bela Lagosi were all lame??? You made fun
of me then for wanting to watch Navy vs. The Night Monsters
or The Blob but I will tell you it is not true that Slime Does
Not Pay and here's how I know:

✡ Noah invited me over this afternoon ✡

he asked me in English and I said yes also in English ha
ha as I don't speak Werbeh

I met him over at the rock and we walked to his house.
He had lost his key so we had to root around under the
snow looking for the fake rock that serves as a key-hiding
locale. There was this wierd chain hanging from a tree and
I whacked into it

"That used to be a tire swing before I broke it," he
explained.

"I like it," I told him politely as I rubbed my battered head. "It makes your yard look tough. It makes it look kinda... Lawn Chainy."

Then he totally cracked up as if I had said the Funniest Thing Ever™ which I kind of in point of fact had

"What did you say?" he shrieked. "Did you say Lawn Chainy? Lon Chaney?"

"Yeah," I said, and then he was laughing so hard I had to offer him his scarf to wipe his nose with.

"I didn't know girls knew who Lon Chaney was," he said.

"I do," I modestly replied. "Creature Double Feature all the way."

"Did Anjali like that kind of movies?" he asked.

"Sure," I lied.

"I watch Creature Double Feature all the time," he said. "I had no idea Anjali did, too."

We found the key then and went inside and he showed me his sofa with the broken springs and the scratchy plaid blanket where he attends to his TV watching. We sat there and watched some bad TV and ate popcorn and man I have to tell you Anjali bad TV was never so good nor popcorn so tasty.

And so that's what I mean when I say that it wasn't a waste at all to watch those movies about the Triphibian Monster or the Terror of Mechagodzilla or the Savage Bees.

"You saw that one????" he asked. "Like when the bees were covering the car and they have to drive into the Superdome and turn down the air conditioning to freeze them off?"

"That very one," I told him. "Anjali and I both watched it." (This is where I skipped over you being miserable and banging your head against the couch and saying when! is! this! cruddy! movie! going! to! be! over!)

"Wow," he said. "So it was kind of like I was watching it with you... like we were in the same time together, just not the same place."

"Well," I said, "3 out of 4 dimensions isn't bad."

That was when he said "huh" and I tried to explain that time is like a 4th dimension to add to our usual 3, but as I was explaining I realized I was totally wrong. We were only together in one of the 4 dimensions, because we were in different places (that's 75% of them) and of course we're always in the same place in the time dimension, because watching the same movie at the same time doesn't actually make us more together in time (unless there's a Creature Double Feature dimension science does not yet know about). But maybe there is such a dimensionality because it did seem like we were closer once we knew we had been watching the Creature Double Feature at the same time.

"Is Anjali in the same place in the time dimension as we are now?" Noah asked suddenly, and that made me think of that wierd idea I had on the bus. I don't know. <u>CAN</u> you move wherever you want in time now? And if that's true, will I be able to find you again when I die? Or will I be wandering around, always missing you, because even when I'm in the right place I'm in the wrong time? I don't like to think that—

"We should make a plan," Noah announced after I tried to explain this. "When we're both dead, we'll meet up again here in my basement at the time when the Savage Bees was on TV, and then we'll all watch it together like we should've last time."

"But WHEN will we meet?" I asked him.

"Like I said, when it was on TV. You'll just have to go back to whenever that was and be here then."

"But what if I don't do it at the same time you do?" I asked. "I mean, what if I die first? Am I supposed to wait around in your basement for like 60 years until you get around to dying?"

"You're not listening," he complained. "I'm not talking about "when" the way we talk about "when" when we're alive when "when" only happens once and then it's gone. I mean the "when" when you're dead and you can travel in time. You don't have to worry about getting there at the same time as me because we HAVE to get there at the same time, because that's WHEN we're meeting, get it?"

I didn't really.

"So if I'm there at that time then it will seem like the time that we're meeting?" I asked.

"That's it," he grinned.

"But that already happened," I objected. "I kind of think I would remember it, if it already happened."

"That's because you were in the wrong place," he explained. "Your brain can't remember it because it hasn't been there yet, but when you get there, then you'll remember that you were there all along."

I told him I still didn't get it, but he said that was because I didn't get the ~~intrackacies intrickisies intrac~~ complications of spacetime.

he might be right

but irregardless, Anjali, now we have a PLAN!!! After we join you in deadness, we're all going to meet in his basement and watch the Savage Bees together under Noah's scratchy plaid blanket.

I can hardly wait!

mjb

P.S. I just thought of something: I guess I should plan to get there a little late to give the two of you some privacy to get to know each other now that you know you like each other and all. But still—can you believe Noah Spivak is making plans with me for after he's dead?????

December 15

I have to tell you, Anjali, that boyfriend of yours is very
FUNNY

We hung out all afternoon after school at 'Niknud Donuts
trying to write a story about these 2 people who are trying
to find each other again after they are dead

at one point due to all the cofee drinking he
announced he had to go to the bathroom but he said
he didn't like to use public restrooms because those
signs that say "employees must wash hands" make him
very enraged

(he thinks he can wash his own hands thank you very
much)

hahhahahahaha

then he was gone and I was there at our table alone
thinking about the fact that he was somewhere else and when

he was somewhere else I was somewhere else for him and that made me think

and then I thought a little bit more about the somewhere else he was being being the bathroom and that made me feel a little embarased like I shouldn't be thinking about that and then he came out having escaped the hand-washing employees and then I told him this mystery of life curtesy of my uncle the toilet-joke writer:

You go to France and you eat breakfast: you're American.

You go to France and you eat lunch: American.

You go to France and go to the bathroom: European!
HAHAHAHAHAHAHAHAHAHAHAHAHAHAHAHAHAHAHA

I had to go home sort of early due to the restriction since the graveyard incident but it was all dark so Noah said I needed an escort and he would walk me. I asked him why he wouldn't need an escort home after he escorted me and then he said he would and that was it then, we were stuck in a loop walking each other back home forever, ha ha ha ha or as they say in Hebrew ah ah ah ah

when we got back to my house my mother wasn't back yet so we went upstairs and suprized Katie who is not so used to seeing me with BOYS in our bedroom. Noah looked around very approvingly at my posters even the Star Wars one in the bathroom. he said he had the same one once

then he sat down on my desk next to my broken typer-writer and looked at all the papers spread there and suddenly I realized what he was going to see and so I jumped over the bed and grabbed him away and said those papers were private

"What the—" he said, panting a little when he got me off his neck, "that was like a half-nelson you put me in!" And he sat there grinning watching me shove all the papers into a drawer

Thank god my mother came home at that moment

I really hope he didn't read anything!!!!!!

I should really start writing to you in Serbo-Croatian

it would be safer if Noah's going to be hanging around here

m

From: Noah Spivak <kulhandlooc@bpm.com>
Subject: Testing, Testing
Date: December 15 7:30:50 PM EDT
To: boxofrain@bpm.com
testing, testing, can you hear me Meredith Beals

From: Meredith Beals <boxofrain@bpm.com>
Subject: RE: Testing, Testing
Date: December 15 7:34:53 PM EDT
To: kulhandlooc@bpm.com
yes yes you;re very noisy
I;m supposed to be doing my homework
for Pritchard and you keep boinging in

From: Noah Spivak <kulhandlooc@bpm.com>
Subject: RE: RE: Testing, Testing
Date: December 15 7:37:12 PM EDT
To: boxofrain@bpm.com
I'm doing the homework too maybe I should
be your tutor since you seem to be confused about
basic punctuation. You seem to be under the
confusion that a ";" is used to indicate something
missing, as in removing the "a" in "you are."

The piece of punctuation you're looking for is an APOSTROPHY, as in "the piece of punctuation YOU'RE looking for is an APOSTROPHY."
The semi-colon is used to separate two linked ideas such as, "Meredith Beals is pretty smart; youAPOSTROPHYd think sheAPOSTROPHYd know how to use a semi-colon."

From: Meredith Beals <boxofrain@bpm.com>
Subject: RE: RE: RE: Testing, Testing
Date: December 15 7:39:24 PM EDT
To: kulhandlooc@bpm.com
hahahahaha

From: Noah Spivak <kulhandlooc@bpm.com>
Subject: RE: RE: RE: RE: Testing, Testing
Date: December 15 7:42:17 PM EDT
To: boxofrain@bpm.com
wow I bet the earth is really grateful that you wasted it;s resources with that brilliant response gotta go

Here's the thing, Anjali. It's really hard to know what someone means when they're doing email. What does that "gotta
go" mean? Was that a "MAN this girl gives me a pain I gotta
get out of here" comment, or a "oh no, the house is on fire,
I better tell Meredith that I have to sign off now before I am
burned to a blackened crisp" kind of "gotta go"?

And now I'm going to sit here and wait for him to call.

That's not as much fun as it looks like in the movies,
you know.

M

PS Anjali I hope you don't think that I meant that I'm a

girl in a movie waiting around for the hero to call or anything

I do totally GET IT that you're the heroine of this story not me and I know that when you and Noah finally get to meet during the Savage Bees in the future past I won't really be part of this story at all

December 16

Anjali, if I ask you something, will you tell me the truth?

Please? Because I really need to know.

Or maybe I don't want to, I don't know.

Do I?

back home

Anjali Anjali I am so so so confused. I need you to tell me what I should think because I think you're the only one I can trust.

Remember I told you awhile ago about how that wierd kid Arnold freaked out in the lunch line that day? How he was just standing there and crying? How it made a big traffic jam because he was blocking the way to the cash register so we all got free lunches to hurry us out of there? That happened again today but wierder.

Arnold was already wailing and wailing by the time I got to the lunch line but instead of the teachers letting us and our free lunches through the end with the cash register like last time this time the whole line was stopped and no one could get by him at all

we were all squished there between the lunch line and the wall and more and more people were coming into the chute behind us and squooshing us some more there was this big commotion up ahead and no one could quite figure out was happening and why no one could get past like we normally can when Arnold freaks

you could hear Walsh in the background trying to get people to stop pouring into the chute and squashing us all to meatloaf you could also hear people up front trying to calm Arnold down but he was uncalmdownable and then I heard someone else up there and though it was too noisy to really hear I thought I heard Wendy Mathinson shrieking "well <u>make</u> him move!" over and over

finally the line behind us let up a little bit and we went backwards and got into the lunchroom with our trays through the exit and then we could see what was going on. It was really wierd. Wendy Mathinson was standing there behind Arnold totally blocking everyone and shaking off Walsh and Morgan-Mack as they tried to get her to move while she kept insisting "well, he has to move! He has to! I want my desert!"

it was like she was so mad at Arnold she could care less about the people behind her but the wierdest part was that you could tell she thought she was right, like it was Arnold's fault and not hers that hundreds of people were getting their lunches all messed up, because she had all the right in the world to stand there and act like a BLEEP because she wasn't getting desert

(fyi the desert wasn't even all that good—it was just jell-o.)

But this is where it stops being funny, Anjali. I was laughing at Wendy along with Lori and Colette and everyone else, but when I looked over to catch Noah's eyes, he wasn't laughing at all. He had this dark angry look on his face like he was furious at her for being such an idiot in front of all those people. That's what I thought, because she did look SO DUMB. Her eyes were all in a fiery blaze and she was almost shaking and suddenly she looked up and saw everyone staring at her and then she really started to shake. That's when I laughed out loud. I laughed and laughed so hard I thought I was going to choke, seeing Wendy standing there and knowing for once what it was like to have everyone laughing at her. But Noah whipped around when he heard me laughing and said, "Don't be a BLEEP, Meredith—" except he didn't say bleep he said the whole B word, and then he walked across that crowded lunchroom full of eyes and put his arm around Wendy Mathinson, leaving me standing there all alone.

I didn't talk to him again until after school. I had kind of assumed that we'd hang out again today so I went outside after the last bell and waited for him to show up, but he didn't. I just stood there, waiting for him, watching everyone else find their friends and go off together and then I was just standing there alone like one of those nature movies where they speed up the tide and it runs down the beach and there's just one lonely rock left there. That was me, the lonely rock on the beach, all alone under the darkening sky, but even then I didn't get it—even then I thought maybe he was waiting for me by the rock on Marrett and even though it was way out of my way I walked across the field, that's how dumb I was.

As soon as I got around the parking lot I could see no one was there but I knew if I turned around someone would see me and know I had thought someone could've been meeting me there so I couldn't go back.

god it's awful when everyone watches you leaving school alone, knowing that it's because you don't have any one to leave school with it just seemed like too much humiliation to bare so I kept on walking past the rock and across the big field

I drifted home alone the long way.

When I got home I realized I was supposed to go see Dartin this afternoon but instead I sat under the water stain thinking about the way Noah looked with his arm around Wendy and saying <u>don't</u> <u>be</u> <u>a</u> <u>b—</u> <u>Meredith</u> and then the phone rang.

"You shouldn't've laughed at Wendy like that," the phone said to me.

That made me mad.

"Why not?" I demanded. "She laughs at <u>me</u> all the time."

"I thought you were better than that," the phone complained. "You shouldn't laugh at people like that. ANJALI wouldn't've laughed at Wendy like that."

"You obviously didn't know Anjali," I snorted. "Anjali TOTALLY would've laughed at Wendy. She would've LOVED to see Wendy get humiliated, because she HATED her."

"You're wrong," the phone insisted. "Anjali didn't hate Wendy."

"What universe are you living in?" I laughed. "Of COURSE Anjali hated Wendy. She DESPISED Wendy—she LOATHED her, just like she should."

"No," said the phone. "I <u>know</u> she didn't. They were <u>friends</u>."

I really had to laugh at that.

"Anjali, friends with WENDY MATHINSON???" I hooted. "That's just the dumbest thing I ever heard of. You're just saying that because you didn't know Anjali. <u>I</u> knew her, and—"

"I knew Anjali," said the phone.

"You didn't know her," I repeated. "You didn't really meet her before she died, that's what you said, and..."

"I never said that," the phone protested. "I <u>wouldn't've</u> ever said that, because I <u>did</u> know Anjali Sen. And I know Anjali was friends with Wendy because that's where I met her first, at Wendy's Halloween Party, back in October. I remember EVERYTHING about that night, because that was the night we started going out."

"What?" I asked, but now I wasn't so much laughing as feeling sick to my stomach. "You and Wendy... you were going out? Are you still going out?"

"Not me and <u>Wendy</u>," the phone said, and that's when it reached out and punched me in the stomach. "Me and <u>Anjali</u>. That's when <u>me</u> and Anjali started going out... and then she died. So don't tell me I didn't know her—I knew her, too. She wasn't only yours."

WOOOOOOOOOOOOOOOOOOOOOOOOOOOOSH

that was the sound of all the air rushing out of the room

it was like the blast when a bomb goes off and all the air

is blown away and the people die in agony

No, I mouthed in the airless silence, nononononononononono

but then the air came back to my lungs in a painful rush

"You're a LIAR!" I shrieked at the phone. "You're lying!!

You're telling a lie, Noah Spivak!!!" And I hung up.

But Anjali Anjali I don't know what happened after because

the next thing I knew I was on the kitchen floor crying though

I have not cried at all since you died but still I laid there and

cried and cried and cried until my mother came home and

found me and now it's 10:57 pm at night and I am still crying.

I don't know why or how to stop it but I do know this:

Noah Spivak is a liar

I KNOW he is Anjali I know you wouldn't—

it's just that I still need you to tell me I'm right

December 17

It's not true, though, right, Anjali? You wouldn't want to be
friends with Wendy Mathinson, would you? ~~and you wouldn't~~
~~go out with Noah Spivak without telling me,~~ not after you
~~know how much I liked~~

I know he's LYING

he has to be lying because I KNOW you would never lie
to me like that

you'd never do that to me you couldn't

you were my best friend!

you're <u>still</u> my best friend!—you promised, <u>remember</u>? You
said you'd be my best friend FOREVER

I hate Noah Spivak

later

Dear Anjali

I'm sitting here staring at my cieling and hating that lying liar Noah Spivak

he just called again

and again

if he thinks I'm ever going to talk to him again he's an idiot as well as a liar.

That's what I told Katie

She has been very useful to me in screening calls and lies to him that I am indisposible at the moment.

As Ms. Pritchard would say she is a very natural prevaricater. She says that's because she has alot of practice lying to boys

it's wierd

I never thought I'd say that Katie understands me but it's true we just had this long talk and afterward we sat on the bed with her arm around me and she rested her chin on my head like she used to do before she outgrew me.

"They all lie, boys," she said. "But on the other hand, why would he lie about Anjali going to a party?"

"Because he's just like Wendy," I sobbed. "He was just being nice to me to make fun of me."

"But it might've been Anjali who lied," she pointed out. "Maybe Anjali lied because she didn't want you to think <u>she</u> was just like Wendy. Maybe she just went to have an excuse to talk to Noah."

I don't think I can explain it to Katie

I can't make myself say out loud the words I am feeling, that if my best friend lied to me about going to Wendy's party then she WAS just like Wendy and if my best friend went and started going out with the boy I liked and didn't even tell me than she was no best friend of mine

but Anjali I know that can't be true it can't IT CAN'T BE because you were PERFECT and my BEST FRIEND and that means Noah is the one who is lying that's true it HAS to be

it can't be any other way.

But here's the thing, Anjali—what I really need in this situation is to talk to my best friend but in case you haven't noticed, my best friend is DEAD.

December 18th

Friday

Dear Anjali,

this is just ridiculous

how is a person supposed to deal with this?????????

My mother is of the mistaken opinion that the best strad-egy is to go to school and get on with my life but what does she know??????

She has no IDEA I can tell you that

The LAST place I can get on with my life is at that school with all those lying liars

God I cannot BARE it with them all looking at me thinking they know

they know NOTHING about me and you can take THAT to the bank to write checks on it the LIARS!!!!!!!!!!!!!!!!!!!

My G-O-D GOD how can they expect

I mean forget it there is just no way

(later)

I didn't go to school. I mean, I went, but when I got there I turned around and walked home. I ended up walking around all day even though the slush was getting into my insufficient shoes

I just kept walking and thinking about all the lying and the dying and about stupid Wendy's stupid party and stupid Noah there laughing at me

What made it worse is that everything's all Christmasy these days which is very incongruous with my mood

Everywhere is all these displays of clean white fake snow in the stores but on the streets the real snow is in clumps of filthy grey

that tells you something about life

it tells you that only what is fake is perfect while what is real pretty much sucks.

Ay!!!!!

There are Christmas decorations in front of all the houses

there are all these thoughtful mechanical deer slowly turning their heads from side to side saying no, no, no

I'm not sure what they're saying no, no, no about.

Maybe they're saying, "You're wrong, wrong, wrong, Meredith" but as to what I am wrong about they are silent.

Then suddenly while I was walking I knew I needed to be back where everything was clear. But I couldn't go back there, because that place doesn't exist anymore. Except that when I thought about it I realized it does. I mean the WHEN was gone, but the WHERE was still there—and 3 out of 4 dimensions isn't bad. So I went back to your house.

Your mother seemed very suprized to see me there standing on the threshhold. She blinked several times behind her glasses and looked a little confused, as if wondering if I'd somehow forgotten about you're being dead but still she invited me in. It was very wierd. Once I was inside it was as if we had no other script to follow and we went right back to the one we always read, where we sat in the living room and she brought out the Mint Milanos and asked after my parents, and that was very wierd, like we were pretending everything was the way it used to be

it sort of seemed that way

The jigsaw puzzle she was working on the last time I was there was still about the same amount undone

one of the pieces had fallen under the table and I picked it up. I didn't like the idea some one would vacuum it up and leave a hole in the picture.

"Anjali would've been so glad you came, Merrydith," your mother said suddenly, saying my name in that funny way she has. That made me feel cheap that she thought I was there for you when really I was there for me. And I <u>was</u> there for me, because you were feeling very far away from me and I needed to know that you were still somewhere, still real, still real the way you were before you died. I needed to be back with the you who never would've gone to Wendy's party, the way you were when you were my best friend sitting in that living room with the Milanos and the jigsaw puzzle and the old record player with the pictures of wierd guys with hairy mustaches on them. But the longer I sat there the more I felt you weren't there either. There were Anjali-shaped holes all over the place in the things that were missing but even more in the things that were still there like that school picture from last year still framed on the TV there you were with your braids and your braces before you cut your hair short and got your new perfect teeth, staring back at me like you were frozen in time

that was the only picture in the room and it will be how they remember you for ever that frozen girl but it wasn't who you were when you died really because then you were more beautiful (beautiful enough that Wendy would invite you to a party so Noah Spivak would notice you)

too beautiful probably to be my friend at all

Then I went to the bathroom to wash my eyes which were burning and then I saw another Anjali-shaped hole because there were only 3 toothbrushes on the wrack

someone had thrown yours out or maybe they buried you with it, like I wanted your mother to do with the Stinky King, and I don't know why but that missing toothbrush made me feel even more miserable than ever and I sat down on the floor and leaned my burning head on the cool of the bathtub and tried not to think about all the times I sat there in the bathroom while you used the funny floss to clean your braces laughing hahaha as if nothing was ever going to make me cry you least of all

198 ♥ MELISSA GLENN HABER

then we would go to your room and talk and talk

or sometimes we didn't need to talk and we might read or you might sit up on your bed and write in your diary the one you kept under your mattress

and then suddenly I needed to see that diary and see what it said I needed to know so I went into your room and there was your bed very neat and under it the diary so I knelt down and slipped my hand between the box spring and the mattress reaching groping for the diary to read what it said: **October 30th: tonight I'm going to betray Meredith.**

It was like I was praying there, my head almost to your blankets as I reached and reached but my fingers touched nothing but mattress and my thumb nothing but boxspring and I sat there trying to remember how to breathe and that was when I saw what was over your bed.

I stood up to get a closer look and saw I was right: it was the Stinky King, the same one I gave your mother so she could bury you with it, and there it was all in a frame with a mat.

I was still looking at it when your mother came in.

"Anjali would've been so touched," she said to me, gesturing to the card.

"That's not what I wanted!!!" I choked out. "I wanted the Stinky King in her <u>coffin</u>! I wanted it with her forever!!!"

"Oh," she said, and then, "Anjali didn't really have a coffin, you know—she was already cremated when you brought the card over."

So I guess that means that when I was sitting on your grave it was on your ashes, just ashes. But where's the rest of you, Anjali? Did you just waft away, like smoke out of a smoke stack, just like smog? I don't like that at all. And I really don't like that the Stinky King didn't go with you. I gave it to your mother because I wanted you to have it so you would know and remember that I was your best friend but when I turned to your mother to say that I was stopped by the misery on her face

it was awful

there was an all-consuming misery there, the kind that is like a fire that burns and burns but never burns away

it is actually amazing to me that a person can live with so much suffering and it made me think about that book we read, about when they used to use curare in operations, back before they knew it did nothing for pain and just paralyzed you frozen instead

That used to really freak me out, that you'd be paralyzed, and they'd be cutting and cutting and you couldn't tell them to stop, and that was your mother, suffering and suffering but not being able to do anything about it

She looked up then and caught my eyes in her curare suffering

"But you must miss her, too!" she said, reaching out and grabbing my hands so hard it hurt, with her long nails digging into me. And then she started to talk, like she'd felt it, too, that you were fading away and she needed to talk about you to keep you with us but the problem was the girl your mother kept talking about wasn't the girl I knew, because she kept saying you were so good and so kind and so perfect, a girl who never did anything wrong, a girl who would never hang up on me when I was feeling bad, or say "Maybe I won't be friends with you if you keep fishing like that" or "You know, Meredith, Noah Spivak is Totally Out of Your League" or going to a party with my worst enemy and probably making out with the boy that I've liked since the FIFTH GRADE because you didn't think I was good enough for him

maybe you were even wearing the costume we made together pepper without the salt OH GOD! When you wore it the next day when we went trick-or-treating it must've had Wendy and Noah <u>ALL OVER IT</u> but still you wore it serenely and didn't say anything to me and like a moron I had no idea

~~and probably the reason I haven't seen your side of the~~ ~~necklace in months is because you threw it out or gave it to~~

and god maybe all those afternoon dentist appointments you claimed were actually lies maybe it was Noah Spivak examining your teeth all those days that last week

God!!!!!!!!!!!!!!!!!!!

maybe you really did keep that a secret even though you always said you never had secrets from me

maybe all you had was secrets from me and I never really knew you at all

that's true probably because the you I remember isn't the same as the one everyone else seems to know and now I'll NEVER know you—

I'll never know if you were the person I thought you were or even if you ever were my best friend in actuality

but now I'm going crazy because that can't be true, <u>right</u>?? You couldn't've been lying to me all those days because you were my best friend! My BEST FRIEND, remember?????? You were the only one who ever knew me and loved me and you can't be disappearing because you PROMISED you would stay here with me here for <u>always</u>

But there are times I feel I <u>can't</u> keep you with me by myself Anjali

I need your help too

it's like the bus is pulling away and I really need you to run faster—

Run faster, <u>please</u>, Anjali, because you're floating away from me the way the smoke breaks up and disappears in the sky and I can't seem to stop it why didn't you tell me?

The doorbell just rang. Katie and my parents were out remedy-ing the no cofee situation so I had to peel myself off the bed and schlump down the stairs to answer it myself. I should've looked out the peephole thing first because when I opened the door it was Noah. I tried to shut it again very rapidly but he shoved his foot inside and then his hand in too and pulled the door back open. He stood there sort of glaring at me, hunching his shoulders inside that yellow rainslicker he has. I guess he's grown since last year because it's getting a little tight on him and it started ripping as he stretched it across his back, so he looked a little like the green and furious Incredible Hulk.

"What the BLEEP is going on with you?" he demanded. "Are you sick or something???"

"I'm fine," I mumbled.

"Then where have you been?"

"I've been around."

"Then why haven't you called me back?" he asked, very furiously.

"Because I thought you'd rather talk to Wendy," I managed.

Noah stared at me and his coat ripped a little more.

"Why would I call <u>you</u> if I wanted to talk to <u>Wendy</u>?" he shouted. "That doesn't make sense at all! If I wanted to talk to Wendy, I'd call <u>her</u> house!"

"Well, you wouldn't find me there, would you?" I shrieked at him. "Because Wendy invites EVERYONE to her house except for me!"

"Look," he interrupted. "I don't want to talk to Wendy—I wanted to talk to <u>you</u>, and I was worried when you didn't call me back, okay?? It's just reminded me—well, you just should've called me back."

I was too occupied by being angry to answer that.

"Look, Meredith…" he said at last. "I wanted to give you something." And he handed me this note, a little shyly. This is what it said:

מרדית אט מית בי ינ אי ליק

"What does it mean?" I asked. "I'm too stupid to read Hebrew, if you don't remember."

"Oh come on, Meredith," he said, ripping the jacket a little more. "You know you're smart." And then he got on his bike and rode away.

So here I am looking at this stupid Hebrew note that's probably insulting me and thinking about the way Noah put his arm around Wendy in the cafeteria while she glared at me, and even when I can remember it's Wendy and not Anjali he was hugging it makes me want to throw up. "You don't understand Wendy," Noah told me, and it's true. I've never understood why she has to be so awful to me and I will never understand why anyone who claims to be my friend could like her. That's the thing. Wendy Mathinson is EVIL and I'm GLAD she was humiliated in front of everyone in the lunchroom because she deserves to writhe in humiliation forever and ever world without end amen and no matter what anyone says <u>I hate her and I hate anyone who ever wanted to be her friend.</u>

That's wierd. I was just rereading that part about how I thought Noah was hugging Anjali and realized it's the first time I've written ABOUT her instead of TO her in the SIX WEEKS since she's died. SIX WEEKS!!!!!! I don't know how I've been able to stand it so long. Six weeks is 42 days. That's 2 days and 2 nights longer than the Great Flood. And at least all those animals on the ark could send the dove off with an olive branch in it's beak and have some hope of peace. Not me. I'm just stuck here and the flood waters are just rising and rising—

Great.

Even thinking about drowning reminds me of Noah.

Monday 21

I hate my life.

I'm such an idiot.

If I hate Noah Spivak so much, why am I always looking for him? It's like I have these broken antennas that cannot be reprogrammed to not pay attention to where he is every moment of the day.

Now he's eating lunch with Wendy.

If Anjali was here, she's probably be eating with Wendy, too.

MEREDITH?

COME ON, MEREDITH!

THIS IS STUPID. WHY DON'T YOU JUST
COME OVER THIS AFTERNOON AND WE CAN
WATCH TV OR SOMETHING? NAVY VS THE SON
OF THE KILLER MECHAZILLA TRIPHIBIAN
NIGHT MONSTER? COME ON, ANJALI!!!! TELL
MEREDITH TO TALK TO ME!

what am I going to do, Anjali?

I can't tell you how much I want to go

I would go anywhere with Noah Spivak, even to the sew-
age treatment plant and that's just the problem

I'd follow him anywhere and then he'd go to Wendy's
party and laugh at me

He's probably laughing at me now that I can't read his
insults in Hebrew

Now he's trying to get my attention across the room,
which is why I have to keep my back turned to him. That's
what I have to do. It's the only way to protect my

WHY IS HE DOING THIS TO ME?????????

why did YOU do that to me, Anjali?

Why wasn't I enough of a friend for you?

December 22

To Whom it May Concern:

I didn't go to school today again I just couldn't. Instead I just sat here all day thinking about how I really don't understand my life at all.

After school Katie came back and sat on my bed with me. She told me my best bet was to give up thinking I can get life at all. She says she's getting an A in psychology in school but failing it in life and the only way to understand people is to assume that they're all very stupid and possibly evil. My mother came in at that point in the conversation and said she thought it would be better if you assumed that other people are well-intentioned but not always fully paying attention to the consequence of their hurting actions. When she left Katie said the only way to understand how our mother could possibly think that was by assuming she is very stupid herself. Personally I'm not so sure. I don't think our mother is actually stupid but it is true that she is very naive. Maybe that's because she's never had her heart broken. She's been in love with my father since they were in high school and he seems to like her back so maybe that's why she's so innocent. That's not like me. I'm only 13 but lately I've had my heart broken twice.

December 23rd

My mother made me go back to school this morning. She drove me to the front steps to make sure I'd go and then she pretty much kicked me out of the car and locked the doors so I couldn't claw my way back in. Then she sat there waiting and waiting for me to go inside while I stood there knowing and knowing I couldn't, because stupid Noah Spivak was blocking the door into school. It was awful. All I wanted to do was turn around and run away from him, because the truth is I can't be near him. Talking to him is like dying a thousand ways at once—it's like I'm choking suffocating my heart being squeezed to pieces all at the same time. I don't know, but I think it might be the feeling of my heart breaking, because I'm beginning to think I might actually be in love with Noah Spivak. I'm not certain, because I have been told love is supposed to feel wonderful but in my case not so much. Instead it's like I'm being pulled in 2 directions at once, because even as I have to run away I have to be with him, and it's ripping my heart in 2. It's like torture or being on the rack or drawn and quartered or mostly it's like an operation with curare and I can't get away because Noah Spivak is coming close to me

"Meredith," he gravels, just liked I used to want to hear but that gravelly voice is like sandpaper on my ears now. "Meredith, will you stop being an idiot for a minute and tell me what we're fighting about?"

"We're not fighting," I choke. "I just hate everything." And I kind of push by him into the school.

"Meredith!" he calls, following me, and the door shuts behind us

(And now we are inside the school and my mother is out-side and even though she is still part of her story she is no longer part of this story as Noah grabs me by the shoulder)

"Don't run away from me," he says, angrily. I—"

"I have to," I mumble. "I just can't do it anymore." And I push my way into the girl's bathroom.

I sat there on the toilet a long time. I guess I was kind

of crying and trying not to which really hurts if you don't know. The worst part was that I couldn't leave because someone came in and was just standing by the sink blocking my escape route. She stayed and stayed and stayed and the breakfast bell rang and finally I had to open the door. That's when I saw who she was. She was Noah.

"You shouldn't be in here!" I told him, but he cut me off: "Well, you shouldn't be mad at me."

I didn't know what to say to that. Sometimes "should" doesn't really enter into it, actually—that's what I've learned lately. I tried to leave, but Noah wouldn't let me go. He was standing between me and the door while he announced: "I'm not going to move until you tell me why you're so mad. Is it because of Wendy?"

I couldn't NOT answer that.

"YES it's because of Wendy!" I blurted out—and that bursting seemed to blow a hole in me so I couldn't keep any of it inside anymore. It all started gushing out of me—the barking—Halloween—tripping me—oh-that's-what-that-smell-is—Anjali—dodgeball—Noah with his arm around her, glaring at me, even though SHE'S the one who stole my best friend and made me look like the jerk when she's the bleeping BLEEP the bleeping B

"She's not a b—" he started, and then I screamed.

"She IS! She is!!!! She is to ME even if she isn't to you and ANJALI knew that and that's why she didn't tell me—she didn't act like I was supposed to like Wendy too because she KNEW what Wendy really is and even if she betrayed me she still hung out with me after, but you're different—even when you pretend to like me you'll only meet me over at the rock and not in front of Wendy or Adam or the rest of them and either that's because you're not good enough to do it, like Anjali was, or it's because you don't like me enough—"

But that was too painful and I had to stop. I just stared at him. I could just catch glimpses of my spazzy hair in the mirror behind him but I couldn't see my ugly blotchy face at all—all I could see was his face changing as I was shrieking. It kind of crumpled.

"You think I'm not like Anjali?"

I didn't answer.

"You think I'm a coward?"

"I didn't say that," I muttered.

"You did say that," he contradicted. And then, "You think I don't like you enough?"

I didn't answer that. There was no answer to that. I have this suspicion that no one can ever like you enough, in the end.

Noah took a deep breath.

"You should've read the note I gave you, Meredith," he said. "I'm not embarased of you. If you'd read the note, you would've known that."

Now I didn't say anything because all I was left with was punctuation marks

" "

?

!

...

¿%?

Suddenly Noah seemed to make up his mind. He grabbed me by the wrist and pulled me down the hall. Wendy and Adam and Zev and all the others were sitting in the Evil Oasis, and when Wendy saw me she took a breath like she was loading her cross bow of insultingness. But Noah stopped her.

"Hey, Zev, Adam—I just wanted to tell you I can't hang out on Saturday, because I'm going to be hanging out with Meredith."

They just stared and stared at him.

I just stared and stared at him.

Wendy just glared and glared at me.

And then Noah Spivak turned to me and grinned.

"Come on, Meredith," he said. "We're going to be late for English."

I don't really have anything else to say right now. I'm just sitting in my room looking at the note he gave me in Hebrew. Here's the thing. Maybe I don't want to know what it says. While I don't know it could mean anything, and maybe I kind of like it better that way.

M

December 24th

Dear Anjali,

It's all snowy snowy outside and very picturesque. In the spirit of the season Katie and I are going to go X-mas shopping although my limited funds are presenting a bit of a problem due to all the recent school-skipping fines. Actually the problem is that they aren't presenting enough hahahah because I only have $28.23 to my name. I guess it's a good thing I don't have to buy anything for you this year! As it is I think it's date-expired chocolates again for everyone. Do you think Noah would like some expired chocolates, too? I hope he has been apprised of the fact that it's the thought that counts, that's all I have to say about it.

Merryxmasdith

(later)

Said Noah is off with his grandparents all day which is making me very miserable. I called him 3 times already but the last time his mother testily reminded me that calling will not get him home any quicker. If he had a cellphone I could call him on that but then again if he had a cellphone I would be sitting around wondering why he wasn't calling ME

Of course maybe he does have a cellphone and I just don't know about it.

Oh great.

Now I have to worry about that, too.

later

I can't believe I wrote that about being glad I didn't need to buy you a present this year. It was a joke, Anjali, really! Joke, Joke, Jokeing, remember?

Please?

Christmas

Dear Anjali,

Merry Christmas, Merry Christmas, fa
flalala
   look at this! I'm typing on my new
TYPERWRITER
   Actually it is my new old TYPERWRITER
   it used to belong to my grandfather
when he was a young man trying to be a
writer in Paris just like Hemingway
   He didn't so much make it--he became
a pharmacist in Preoria instead
   Anyway we had such a nice day
   For some reason Katie and I woke up

wicked early like at 5:50, just like we
used to when we were kids

I looked at her and she was awake and
she looked at me and I was awake and
then we both jumped up

we went skittering down the stairs
and she made cofee

I drank a cup too because I'm
sofisticated like that though Katie
commented it is more sofisticated to
use less milk and less sugar and to
love the bitter blackness--that is the
point to cofee and to life that's what
she says

the X-mas tree looked very pretty
against the frost-flecked windows and
there were all sorts of packages under-
neath including a square one that kind
of matched the paper bag Katie had at
the mall yesterday from the store where
they do not so much sell calandars with

cats on them as albums from groups like the GREATFUL DEAD

then katie turned on the x-mas tree lights and we sat there drinking our cofee and opening our stockings because we;re allowed to do that part before breakfast

there was all the usual good stuff like the chocolate and the peppermint and the orange into the toe and a deck of cards my dad picked up at the Cleveland airport that say CLEVELAND'S ON A ROCK'N'ROLL on them

there was also the usual joke piece of coal that is actually stale licorish (if it's coal it's pretty good, but if it's licorish it's terrible!)

then my parents came down with the usual complaint that we were up too early and we all had another cup of cofee together before my grandmother and aunt and uncle and cousin Whitney came

Whitney is the one I told you about, the one my grandmother says is "her own person"

she is her own person in that way where she has shaved her head and has all sorts of earrings in her face as we used to say 17 of them to be exact including one through each nostril

it turns out hair is very enhancing for her as her head is kind of a funny shape but my Aunt Lisa says the baldness and the piercing is fine as long as Whitney is happy.

You could tell my grandmother disagrees.

she is very old fashioned and has a firm girls-should-have-hair-and-only-wear-earrings-in-their-ears policy

When we opened the presents my grandmother kept cracking wise that she hoped someone would give Whitney a wig

Katie handed me her small square pack-age with a big big grin

I opened it with a big big grin

Hello, "American Beauty" by the Greatful Dead

My other presents were pretty good too and everyone seemed to appreciate the Whitman's chocolate samplers and did not seem to mind that they were expired

Then we sat around the piano and Whitney played x-mas carols while we all sang

Whitney might look bald and funny what with all the metal studded around her muzzle but she is actually very tal-ented at the piano

even my grandmother had to begrudg-ingly admit it which is very unusual for her as she generally is more com-fortable being critical.

After everyone else left we had our

usual dinner of turkey + stuffing + cranberry sauce sandwiches and watched "It's A Wonderful Life" on the TeeVee. That was when you used to come over and my father would make his dumb and probably racist comments about Indians coming over on Thanksgiving, not X-mas and then we'd all watch TeeVee together. This year you weren't ringing the door- bell but I was sort of hoping Noah might come by as he's another one who does not attach so much importance to December 25 the heathen but it turns out he and his family always go to the movies on X-mas. So that's where he is, and maybe that's why you haven't been showing up around here, either. I don't blame you. I guess I'd be off with him at the movies too if I had the chance.

Huh.

I just realized something. If you were

alive now, you probably really WOULD
be off with him now, because he really
would be your boyfriend

 i guess that means too I wouldn't be
hanging out with him tomorrow either
 huh.

                                        (later)

My mother just came upstairs with one more present.
It was a tiny box and when I opened it up there was
a gold necklace inside. I guess I must've put my hand
up to the BEST AR FOR necklace because she kind
of flinched.

 "No, no," she said. "I don't want you to wear this instead
of Anjali's necklace—I bought it FOR Anjali's necklace."
And she took the old crusty chain off me and strung the
BEST AR FOR charm on the beautiful new golden links and
clasped it back around my neck.

 "There," she said, her hands on my shoulders. "Now

you won't get neck gangreen and die." She pulled me close. "I don't want you to get neck gangreen," she whispered, and for the first time I knew what your death had meant for her.

December 26

Noah just called. We were thinking about
going skating but he says the red light
is on at the pond so unless we want to
end up drownded like Kristi Lawrence we
can't go. Instead he wants to go sledding down the hill next to it.

Do you remember when my father tried
to get us to go down that hill and
you totally freaked? I'll tell you this
Anjali: some things have gotten smaller
as we've gotten bigger but that hill is
not one of them. So anyway I'll write
when I get back--if the hill doesn't
kill me, that is.

(Actually, if the hill does kill me, I
guess I'll talk to you alot sooner)

your best friend,
meredith

PS I'm putting on "American Beauty" for you to listen to while
I'm gone. Hope you like it!

later

Dear Anjali

sorry about that--the doorbell rang and
I didn't have time to finish. So we went
sledding and it was pretty fu

December 27th

Dear Anjali

~~December 28th~~

~~Dear Anjali~~

Dear God

You might not know me, but I'm Meredith
Beals, one of Your human beings?
 i don't know who else to write to.
 i can't really say this to Anjali
though she probably knows without my
telling her.
 She probably knows EVERYTHING
 that's the problem she's watching me
AL LTHE TIME and now she knows I'm the
worst friend ever
 but here's the thing
 she wasn't the only one who liked him
 i liked him too
 i liked him FOR TWO YEARS before she
did but when she said she might want to

like him herself i said it was okay

i said she could have him and i would step aside but i never really meant it i only said that because i knew i didn't have a chance with him but i didn't really think she did either but here's the thing: i never wanted him to be HER boyfriend

it would've been a rusty spike nailed into my head to see them together

i mean i didn't so much mind her LIKING him too when we both just talked about him all the time but still i never thought she'd go DATE him or anything I mean since she was MY BEST FRIEND I never thought she'd try and actually be the girlfriend of th boy she knew i liked

or maybe i wasn't her best friend at all, just someone she kept around to feel even more beautiful and popularer in contrast

sometimes i felt that way, that she was always feeling superior to me and

liking it like when we went shopping
together and she would make us both try
on the same outfit's

we would stand there in the dressing
room and I'd have to see how much better
everything looked on her and she'd be so
beautiful even under the flickering ugly
lights while I'd be one big lumpy splotchy
zit with spazzy frizzy hair tree trunk
legs flat 2 by 4 chest, with her all perfect next to me, leaning on my shoulder
and smiling as if someone was taking our
picture BFF best friends 4 eva

as if

if she really WAS my best friend she
would've gotten it that i liked him
first, that i REALLY liked him

but instead she acted like that didn't
matter, like she had a right--
she didn't think about me at all.

And that makes me think she was NEVER

thinking about me because she went and made herself his girlfriend and didn't even tell me before she up and DIED

But I don't know what to do about that now which is why I need to talk to You what happened last Saturday. I mean I have gathered God that You are pretty omnicient and that You probably know what happened but maybe You don't know what happened from my point of view so that's why I have to tell You

it was Saturday morning and I was waiting for Noah to come get me for the sledding but then while I was waiting I went back upstairs and put on this music for Anjali because I wanted her to stay there in my room and not follow me and Noah for once. And that was when I suddenly figured out this awful thing, that I was about to go sledding with my dead best friend's boyfriend.

And I got it then that the only reason
I was getting a chance to go sledding
with him was because she was dead, and
that made me feel like maybe I was acting happy that she had died. But God
that's not what I thought. I'm not happy
that she's dead at all AT ALL and I've
been meaning to talk to You about that
because I'm still really angry about
it like so angry that I've never been
angrier except that I'm also angry at
her and I don't know what to do about it
God because then the doorbell rang and
I went down stairs and there was Noah
with his sled strapped to his back so he
looked like a turtle

I don't know if You know Noah

he is Jewish but I think we still have
the same God or something so maybe You
know him too he's this boy I've known
a couple of years and I've kind of had

this crush on him for a really long
time. At first I liked him because he's
really really cute but lately I've disc-
overed he's funny and nice and good to
be with too and we have alot in com-
mon and I don't know, God, but I've
never felt the way I feel around him.
And now he's coming to my house with
his sled on his back, standing next to
his bike and telling me to go get mine
bcause the hill is really far away but
I told him a lie (sorry) that my bike
is broken because I didn't want him to
know I don't really know how to control
a bicycle appropriately in the snow
and then he said he would give me a
ride

I got all embarased at that and said I
was too fat and he said MEREDITH YOU'RE
NOT FAT and then he told me to put the
sled on my back and climb on behind

him and hold on. I had to lock my arms
around his waist to keep from falling
off and this is really embarasing to
talk about with someone like You God
but it was like I was hugging him, and
I've never hugged a boy before

i wish I could explain it but the only
thing I can think of was that it felt
very ALIVE. Noah felt very ALIVE with his
muscles moving under his coat and with
his breathing and the heat that came off
him and all I could think with the rythm
of the bike was HE'S ALIVE and I'M ALIVE
ALIVE and that felt very important, like
the most importantest thing that ever was

it felt important especially because
the day was so COLD and so very covered
with snow

maybe at that moment we were the only
alive things in all Your world

that's how it felt as we stood at the

top of that steep hill, looking down
to the one red spot that was the light
that told you not to go out on the pond
unless you wanted to end up drownded

and then Noah launched himself down on
the sled, sliding and skidding and skittering down the slope and then wiping out
at the bottom near the pond, his red ski
jacket just a splotch of red down there
in all that white. And i was laughing too,
laughing so hard I worried I'd forgotten
how to breathe and then I lost my foot-
ing and I slipped part way down the hill,
and I was still trying to stand up when
Noah came trudging up the hill and then
it was my turn and I threw myself down on
the sled and going so fast it almost blew
my eyelids off bouncing thump bump thump
bump bone jarring bump and then a little
leap and over into the snow and maybe I
was screaming I don't know I couldn't hear

because of the voice in my head shouting
I'M ALIVE I'M ALIVE I'M ALIVE I'M GLAD I'M
ALIVE and then I was lying there in the
snow and looking up at the clouds racing
past the sun small and remote in the winter sky and the red light next to the pond
and the red spoltch that was Noah yelling
for me to bring the sled up

    then he took another turn

    I took another turn

    the whole time there was a shouting
in my ears I'M ALIVE I'M ALIVE I'M ALIVE
to the accompaniment of the shrieking
of the wind

    Noah tried sledding standing up

    he almost broke his neck

    I tried sledding backwards

    I ended up in the bushes

    I kept falling while I was coming up
the hill and Noah was laughing and then
suddenly he asked,

"Do you feel bad laughing, when Anjali is dead?"

I stopped laughing then, because in truth I did feel bad. My necklace had come out of my coat and gotten all cold and it burned against the skin of my chest when I tucked it back in. Anjali felt very close at that moment, and God, i didn,t want to say it, but it's true: I didn't want her there, not then. And then I remembered being up on the Ferris wheel with her, when she said she'd always let me sit there with her and Noah. But now I know it's not true. I know that boys do get in the way, and girls do, too--I know that now, because Anjali was getting in the way and I hated it.

Noah could feel her there too.

"Listen," he said. "About Anjali...."

But I didn't want to talk about Anjali.

"No really," he insisted. "I want you

to know this. You were right, Meredith. I know Anjali knew Wendy was mean to you, because she told me I should tell Wendy to lay off you, remember?"

So that was Anjali who said those words: DON'T BOTHER MEREDITH. SHE'S OKAY. Knowing that made me feel worser than ever.

"I did that for her," Noah said. "I wanted to do that for her, because she was so pretty, and so nice... it was like almost the last thing she ever said to me. She said it when she hung up, and then she wasn't in school that Friday, and then she never called me back. NO ONE called me back until you did that night, and just announced she was dead..." And then he started to cry.

That was when I knew I was WRONG about everything

I mean I've been hoping Anjali isn't

totally still Noah's girlfriend but at that
moment I knew she was and that her supposed best friend was betraying her just
like I was mad at her for betraying me

but here's the truth--I might;ve been
betraying her, but she kind've started
it because she KNEW i liked Noah Spivak
first and for forever and even though
she knew that, she was his secret girlfriend and never told me

and besides it's not FAIR that even
though she's DEAD she's keeping me from
him it's like she's keeping them BOTH
from me and if i don't have either of
them I really have nothing

That's what I was thinking as I sat
there looking over the white white world.

Noah felt it, too, the sadness, and
then he shook his head and grabbed me
with his snowy mitten.

"I want to take one last trip," he said.

"Go ahead," I managed to choke.

"No," he said. "I mean I want to take one last trip together. Come on--sit down in front."

So I did, and then we were off down the hill.

It was amazing, that trip. It made me very happy that I was living in this strange world You made

we took the longest path and soon we were going fast

everything was a white blur

we were jostled and jumbled up and down and I banged my chin so hard I thought my teeth would break and still it was so great that all I could hear was I'M ALIVE I'M ALIVE (but under that a rattle tattle yayayayayayaya and then a big bump and Noah flew off behind me)

I kept flying

the sled sped on and on and on

it was going so fast time was

s l o w i n g down

and then I was going faster than the
speed of light

I was going so fast time was going backwards

I could feel myself getting younger
and younger

--Anjali was still alive--

--we were talking about Noah--

--then I was back on the top of the
hill with Anjali--

--we were 8 and my father was trying
to coax her down--

--she wouldn't go--

--we were under the blankets telling
our secrets--

--she was saying that i was the only
one who really knew her--

(and then a snow bank coming)

I closed my eyes

screaming

Noah was screaming behind me

then the impact

white white white

(they say you see a white light when
you die)

then stillness, silence

am I about to see you, Anjali? Someone
is calling my name, I blink

"Meredith! Meredith! Don't move! Don't
stand up!"

I blink and turn my head. Noah's
behind me, red on white, racing down
towards me and I'm

I'm

I'm on the

I'm on the deep and not quite frozen pond where Kristi Lawrence broke
through and died

and not far beneath me is the dark
cold water

and not far beneath me is death

and though my heart is shrieking I'M
ALIVE! I'M ALIVE I know that's just what
Kristi Lawrence thought just before she
broke through and what Anjali thought
before she--

(it turns out being alive is not something you can count on forever)

Noah is making these wierd sounds behind
me as if he's crying but he calls "it's okay
it's okay Meredith" but the ice was creaking and moaning and i was moaning too

"You just have to keep your weight
spread out," he calls, and then I know he
means I'm too fat the ice can't hold me

"I'm too heavy!" I call but he says
"Come ON Meredith, I TOLD you you're not
fat" and then "I'm coming to get you!"
and then he started creeping out on the
ice lying flat and inching forward and
when he got close he grabbed me by the
mitten and pulled

and then we were on the bank, both panting, the ice behind us creaking and Noah was calling my name, and then God I didn't mean it to happen, I swear I didn't, but I turned towards him and then he was kissing me

and I was kissing him back (and I've never kissed a boy before)

And then Noah was pulling away and burying his face in his hands. And I knew why, because I felt it too, that Anjali was there, closer than ever, and I could feel she was furious her fury burning the snow that I was kissing her boyfriend and her boyfriend was kissing her best friend but God I knew then that was what the singing meant when I heard it I"M ALIVE I"M ALIVE in my ears

it meant that Noah and I were ALIVE and that Anjali's just not

she's not

but here's the thing God, the thing i
need to know

either Anjali's here seeing me cheat
with her boyfriend

or if it's not cheating that's because
she's GONE just like everyone says she is

and I really can't handle either one,
God

because it isn't fair either way

and it isn't fair that Anjali

it was NEVER fair that Anjali

because here's the thing, God, why
SHOULD she be mad at me? Because I
liked him FIRST and SHE KNEW IT and just
because she was beautiful and perfect
that doesn't mean that I shouldn't--

and besides she wasn't always perfect, she really wasn't

YOU know she wasn't

You know there were times she was lazy
and times she was mean she could be

very mean to me sometimes and I let
her because I was always amazed she was
willing to be my friend when she was
sosmartsoprettysofunnysogreat. And she
knew that about herself, that she was
sosmartsoprettysofunnysogreat and there
were times this fall I know she thought
that she was too good for me, I know
it. And I know she thought Noah was too
good for me too, because she told me I'd
never have a chance, and that's why she
should get to like him. But here's the
thing: she should've let me have the
chance. I SHOULD'VE had the chance, and
you really could've let me, you know,
for once you could've thought about me
because i think you didn't really think
about me all that much lately i think you
took me for granted--sometimes I think
you never thought about me at all

I've never said that before, and I

guess maybe I shouldn't say it now but
I can't help it. That's how I feel, and
I've felt that way a long while now

but you shouldn't be reading this,
anyway, Anjali

it's private

December 29th

I've been sitting here all morning and
remembering this time when I was nine I
was fighting with Anjali and I ended up
under the dining room table crying and
mourning that we would never be friends
again. I remember how my mother came
and told me it was okay, and then she
reminded me of all these other times we
fought which I have to admit were kind
of alot because we were not exactly pac-
ifists, Anjali and I

but then my mother reminded me too
of all the times we made up which were
alot also and that made me realize she

was right and that me and Anjali were more than friends--we were practically sisters. And that meant it was okay that we were sometimes fighting, because our friendship was too big to fail.

But here's the thing: it's different now, because now I don't know how to make up with her. I don't even know if she's here to fight with me, much less make up again/ And there are days I don't even know WHO this person is that I'm fighting with--and the worst part is I might not ever know any more.

Noah keeps saying that when you're dead you can go anywhere in the WHEN of time but I feel that that's exactly what I can't do with Anjali

when Anjali was alive I could go with her into the past and try to figure out what had happened but now that she's gone it's like she took the past with her

Now I'll never know what she was
thinking when she went to Wendy's party
and kissed Noah

Now I'll never know what she was
thinking in the Ferris wheel when she
claimed she'd be my best friend forever

Now I'll never know what she thought
about me at all.

Sometimes I think I'm really losing her

sometimes I think we're not remembering the real her only the her we want
to remember

for her mother that means remembering
a girl who was always perfect

ditto for Noah

but I can't remember that girl because
that's really not who she was

if I remember her like a white mar-
ble statue I really will have lost her
forever

Because you WEREN:T always perfect to me Anjali you know you weren't

and I need to remember the WHOLE you and that means remembering you went to WEndy's party and knowing you thought you deserved Noah more than me

I need to remember that there were lots of times you just weren't what I needed you to be because that in fact is part of who you were

but I just don't know what to do with that now that there's no way for that to change.

This morning Katie came into our room and kind of flopped on my bed.

"So," she said. "Is this Noah guy your boyfriend?"

"No," I told her, and then, "I think he might still be going out with Anjali."

"Huh," she said. "That's awkward."

One thing I have to say about that Katie is that she is very practical with her many years of experience. In her estimation Noah and I need to Talk which is something I am not so sure about. I mean the last time I saw him he had just biked me home after we had sat in a field of snow crying and crying and getting chilblains on our cheeks. Since then we have talked a little on the phone but it has been very wierd. I mean I like to hear his voice but I can't really find anything to say so I keep hanging up but then as soon as I do I want to call him again--it's like wanting to eat just one more piece of candy even when you are not in point of fact, hungry, which makes me think I might actually be addicted to Noah Spivak.

today when I called him first (I think it's been like 5 times) his mother recognized my voice and said "Hi, Meredith--Noah's on his way out the door but I bet he'll want to talk to you" and then Noah got on the phone and told me he's going out to see a movie with Zev and Wendy Mathinson and maybe i should come too

that was when I told him I had more

intriguing plans like being ripped to
shreds by dobermans while having rusty
spikes nailed into my head

that was when he said I should rethink
my priorties and that he'd call me
afterwords

so then he went to the movies and
called me (that was conversation #2) and
we talked some more then I called him
back (#3) and he said we should meet
at Dunkin' Donuts which we did (skip-
ping (#4) when I had to call back to ask
which Dunkin' Donuts he meant)

mostly we just talked about the movie
and the dobermans and then we went out
and walked in the cold

man the cold is so cold with the
freezing of the boogers and the chilblains on the cheeks and also on the
hands when you;ve lost your mittens and
didn't get new ones for Christmas. But

we walk together through the cold and Noah says,

"You should've come to the movies, you know."

That is when I told him I would not go ANYWHERE with Wendy Mathinson for a million billion dollars in cold hard cash.

"You just don't know her," he said. "She's okay."

"No she's not," I told him. "You don't get to be nice if you're only nice to people you like. And she is not nice to me. She tripped me EVERY SINGLE day in 5th grade when I had to hand out the paper, and she always told everyone not to touch my books because they had nerd germs on them...."

"Aw, come on," he said. "That's stupid stuff. It--"

"It's not stupid when it's YOU," I told

him. "And that's not all, there was this time when we had to be partners in ballroom dancing and she stomped on my toe on purpose and broke my foot."

"She broke your foot????"

He was kind of missing the point.

"Well she didn't exactly BREAK it, but she sprained it... and Anjali saw and she kicked Wendy in the leg and got detension for it--she got that detension for me. But even that's not it. It's not all those little things--it's everything all together. I guess you just kind of had to be there."

"Maybe she'll be nicer to you if she gets to know you," Noah tried, but I told him that if a leper can't change her spots she can always wait for them to fall off. He laughed then and his Andean mitten brushed my chilblained hand

We didn't talk too much after that,

but even that was okay. We just walked through the cold and frosted world over to Gladden with the swinging of the strings from his hat keeping rythm to our walking and then we sat on the creaky creaking broken swings and finally I say to him, to Noah Spivak

"Can I ask you something?"

His gravelly voice is husky when he says yes.

"Are you still going out with Anjali Sen?"

Now Noah stops and looks at me and the strings that hang from his hat are still while his Andean mittened hands are close to mine, very close

"I don't know, Meredith," he says to me. "Am I?"

And that was the moment the chain on the swing gave out just like I always said it would and I ended up sprawling

on the ground with Noah jumping next to
me to make sure I was not in point of
fact concussed

   and even though he didn't really
answer his own question in words after
that from other evidence I think have a
pretty good idea.

                     m

P.S. I looked up the word "chilblains"
in the dictionary. That's not what I
have.

Due to the magic of the internet I just figured out what the Hebrew in Noah's note says: ekil I uoy eb thgim ti htiderem.

This is what Noah said when I told him I'd read it:

"Well, you took long enough."

"Well," I pointed out, "it WAS in Hebrew."

"Well," he pointed out, "I figured you were smart enough to get past that."

"I'm smarter in English," I told him, but then I was feeling shy so I told him I had to get off the phone. As soon as I did I wanted to call him back but it was just as well I didn't because Katie and I

had to go to the mall to return the ugly
matching sweaters our grandmother gave us
for X-mas. Noah's planning to come over
tonight for New Year's Eve so I was going
to use my X-change $ to buy him his own
X-mas copy of "American Beauty" so he can
listen to some good music for a change but
before that Katie wanted to go buy some
minute piece of miniscule clothing in one
of her stores. I used to think Katie only
bought uniforms for s tupid people but now
I guess I am wrong because even though
the clothing is sort of stupid Katie turns
out to not be so dumb after all so don't
judge a book by it's abbreviated cover.
Anyway I did not try anything on as it is
not exactly My Scene but instead drifted
around the racks while Katie was in the
dressing room. And then guess who was
there? Can you? Da dat dat da of course:
the QUEEN OF THE STUPIDS, WENDY MATHINSON

She came over to me all mad and squinty.

"You shouldn't think you're all special because Noah Spivak's been hanging out with you," she hissed at me by way of greeting. Then she pulled close so I could see the lettuce between her beaver teeth. "Everyone KNOWS that Noah Spivak doesn't like YOU, he likes ME."

Here's the funny thing: suddenly I wanted to laugh out loud because I knew she'd lost her superpowers over me. I don't know how, but it was as if I'd been given the bullets and bracelets and the Eye of Agamoto and the antirepulser ray and Letterman's Silent E and the cloak of impenetrability since the last time I saw her and they were all making this protective shield around me and from that fortress I could only laugh at her measley attacks. But that made her madder than ever

"HE DOESN'T LIKE YOU!!!!" she shrieked,

as if we were the only people in the mall. it's funny about Wendy that she's so self-centerd and selfish that she doesn't mind making a MORON of herself in public, standing there shrieking "NO ONE LIKES YOU!!! NO ONE!!!! NO ONE EVER LIKED YOU, YOU UGLY DOG!!!!" She was nearly chocking on her exclamation points and that made me crack up too because it was at that very moment that I finally GOT what dopey Dartin had been trying to say to me, back when he was telling me that it was important that Anjali CHOSe me. I got it then, and it's true. Anjali DID choose me and practically the last thing she did on earth was to ask Noah to tell Wendy to leave me alone.

"You're wrong," I told Wendy proudly. "ANJALI SEN liked me. I was her best friend."

"Anjali Sen is DEAD!" she spat, trying

to be mean, but she couldn't do it, because friendship is like a cloke of impenetrability and the Eye of Agamoto and all the rest, and because that stupid Dartin was right--I didn't lose it when Anjali died: she CHOSE me, and Wendy Mathinson can't take that away. So I stood there laughing and she stood there sputtering until Katie came out of the dressing room looking all tall and gorgeous and perfect even in her uniform from the stupid-person store. When she saw me there with Wendy she came over and kind of draped her arm over my shoulder.

"So is this one of your friends?" she drawled.

"Not exactly," I said. "THIS is Wendy Mathinson."

"OH," said Katie significantly, looking Wendy up and down with devastating unimpressededness. "Of course it is. Well, come on, Meredith--let's go. We need to get you something gorgeous for whatshis name when he comes over tonight."

And so I waved goodbye to Wendy, and my sister and me rode off into the sunset, wrapped in our clokes of impenetrability.

So now I'm home, waiting for Noah to come over, but mostly I'm thinking about you, Anjali. And this is what I've been thinking. You DID choose me, even if I'll never know why. You chose me back when we were 4 years old, back when it was love at first sight. And it WAS love at first sight, and I feel sorry for anyone who would be embarased to say that, because it's true.

I loved you.

I loved you, and I think you loved me too. And even if I'll never know if you loved me as much as I loved you, and even if I'll never know WHY you loved me at all, I know that you did. And no one can ever take that away.

And this is what I'm thinking, too, Anjali, that maybe I've been wrong to think you've been disappearing because no one else remembers the same Anjali that I do. Because maybe no one else CAN know the Anjali I knew, because the Anjali I knew was the Anjali-with-Meredith, and no one else could know it, because no one else was me. It is like what your dad was saying about the colors: maybe I saw a different blue when I looked at you than Noah did or your mother did not just because I see dif-ferent but because you WERE a differnet blue with me than you were with every-one else, like Wendy is a different blue with Noah--maybe that explains why he doesn't hate her (but that doesn't mean I don't have to hate her too because for the record I still hate her forever)

So that's what I'm thinking, as I'm listening to that Greatful Dead song "Ripple"

no one else can know what it was for me to be your friend becuse

that path is for (rest)

your steps alone

It's like what I was saying at your funeral, even though I didn't understand it then. No one can understand who you were with me like I can--you really had to be there. But here's the thing, Anjali: I understand, because I WAS there--and I'm so glad I was.

love, your best friend
Meredith

December 31st midnight

so the ball has dropped and started another year. Everyone else is standing around downstairs saying the usual things about being amazed another 12 months are gone, and wondering that global warming and squid flu haven't done us all in yet. Katie's down there drinking champagne and sharing in the hilarity but I'm sitting up here under the water stain writing and thinking about how we didn't all escape disaster

you didn't, I mean, and that means I didn't entirely either

Except that I'm still here

and except that I just hung up the phone with Noah Spivak.

He was supposed to come over tonight but there's this big snowstorm so he was stuck at his house instead so we've been talking on the phone since 9:21.

It was a good conversation

mostly we talked about you and but also about me and about Lon Chaney and farting in the linen closet and suing the town for the Gladden swing to the head and about what we might do together in the new year. It's not exactly like being on the phone with you but it is a little bit the same and the ways it's different are not exactly worse it's mostly just a little confusing

I don't know

Maybe Wendy's right and Noah doesn't really like me

or maybe really he still likes you and is still your boyfriend

but then again maybe he does like me for real

or maybe he doesn't now but he will later—

it's a new year and everything is possible.

But here's the thing: when we said the countdown and shouted happy new year together I think—that is I think—that Noah Spivak kissed the phone good night

January 1

Mt. Auborn Cematary

Dear Anjali

So I got up really early this morning. Katie and my parents were still asleep so I just left them a note on the table and slipped outside with my fountain pen and my leather diary in my pocket.

Outside everything was all bowed down with the weight of the storm. The big branch from the pine tree next to our house was all curved down over the walkway, like it was an archway over our door into a world of white.

It was very beautiful, the world, very still and quiet, fresh and waiting, like a new white piece of paper.

Last night Noah asked if he could come with me today but I'm glad I came alone. Now instead of talking I'm getting to feel this strange feeling. I'm not sure what to call it or even if it has a name at all, but maybe I don't really need to know it's name right now. I guess part of living is knowing you can't understand it all and knowing that's okay. Or at least that's what I was thinking as I came through the big gates of the cematary.

My feet made these contemplative crunching sounds in the slush as I made my way to your grave and even the feeling of my boots in the slush felt very significant

I don't know why

maybe it was because it was so actual and real

maybe it was because it was an insignificant detail and in the end insignificant details are all we've got.

And that's what I've kind of been thinking today. You were details to me, Anjali, a thousand actual and tiny details, even if I can't sum them up into one or even a thousand DESCRIBING WORDS. Maybe that's why the words on your gravestone make so much sense to me. The stone's finally there now with your name and date and then just a little sentence that sums it all up: "Words fail." It's true. Words do fail, and memories do, too, but still time goes on and I think it goes backwards as well as forwards. The past is still real, I mean, still there, and that means no one can take it away.

It's hard to say what I mean. I'm not trying to say that it's there because I'll always remember—it's more than that. I mean that even when I get all senile and forget you and even when I join you in death the past will still exist because it WAS. It just IS and IS REAL and EXISTS even if no one remembers it, that's what I think. And to me that means no one can take those years away. And even if you had lived and decided Wendy Mathinson was your new best friend and that you were lame for ever thinking I was worthy to be your friend, all those years when you WERE my best friend couldn't be erased, because they are THERE and they will ALWAYS be there, even if we don't know how to travel back to get to then yet.

It's like the tower. Remember when Noah and I got lost here, and could only figure out where we were by getting into the 3rd dimension to look down on the other 2? Well I guess we need a 4th dimension to make sense of our 3 dimensional world, and that dimension is time. But that must mean we need a 5th dimension to make sense of the time one, and maybe it's true that that dimension is death. And maybe that means that after I go senile and after I die I'll find myself floating above it all and seeing my past spread out like a map. And if that's true then I can float over it and find that place in space and time where you and I met that first day, that day when we hid behind our mother's legs and peeked out at one another, back in the beginning

And maybe I'll float a little further and see us all those other times, doing each other's nails or chasing each other in the Gladden playground or sitting on the broken swings or playing Spit reading each other's diaries knowing each other inside out blue apples both together

I might float to Wendy's party

I might see you and Noah there and even though I hate it and it hurts it's also there and true—but also there and true is that you told Noah to take care of me

and maybe I'll float back to the day we sat in my living room watching the Savage Bees

and that will remind me of my promise, and I'll float further in space to where Noah's watching the same movie under his scratchy scratchy blanket, and maybe you'll be there too, waiting, and we'll see each other again and scream and squeal

or maybe we'll be old ladies and maybe we'll have grown apart or maybe you'll still be mad because it turns out Noah became my boyfriend or maybe I'll still be mad because it turns out Noah always stayed your boyfriend but even then Anjali it won't really matter, because the future can't change the past. It's still there, always the same way, with little Meredith and little Anjali peeking out behind their mother's legs. It was love at first sight, that's what every one said, and it will always be love at first sight, no matter what happened or might have happened after.

And that means something to me, Anjali

It means that somewhere somethere somewhen you and I are still together

It means nothing that has been is ever truly lost

It means the world can still be beautiful even though I really really miss you

It means I might still be happy.

And Anjali it means something else, too. It means that even though I miss you so much it hurts and even though I'm

freezing my BLEEEEEEP off I still feel content right now—
not because of Noah, but because of YOU. I'm SO GLAD
you chose me as your friend, Anjali Sen, because I chose you,
too, and I choose you now to say you have my promise that
I will ALWAYS choose you. You will always be part of me, no
matter what else happens, and you can take THAT to the
bank and write a check on it, because you know I will always
be there in the past and in the future writing check after
check signed by your best friend,

Meredith Jane Beals

ACKNOWLEDGMENTS

This book is a work of fiction, but fiction is rooted in fact—and the fact is that I had a best friend when I was 13 years old. Her name was Jessica Lee Garfinkel, now Jessica Keteyian, and I will always be grateful that she chose me as her bent pinky. Certain other people from that time—perhaps a particular good-looking boy who used to fart in the linen closet while we talked?—might also recognize themselves if they happen upon this novel, but it is to Jess that I dedicate this book.

Four other people from my present also deserve my always gratitude for bringing this book to life: my best friend and traveling companion, Ezra Glenn, who even 25 years ago was so amusing that I once threw a burning toaster oven into the snow rather than get off the phone with him; my patient agent, Erin Murphy; Jessica Handelman, who brought this book to such beautiful physical form; and, of course, my insightful and supportive editor, Liesa Abrams—thank you most of all.

I also want to acknowledge the early kid readers for their help and comments: Mattie Glenhaber, Jeremy Astesano,

Davis Downie, and Samira Teixeira. Here's also a tip of the hat to Ray Coffey for the Lawn Chainy comment. I of course need to thank the friends who have always put up with the very boring ups and downs that go with writing, especially Peter Bebergal, Sarah Bennett-Astesano, Jennifer Costa, and Kate Horsley. Special thanks have long been owed to Hilary Rappaport for her friendship and ongoing support of my books. I am also continually grateful to my writer-aunt, Ellen Larson, for all of her help and advice; to the Reverend Robert Wexelblatt for being my writerly mentor since I was about four; to the Commonwealth School; to my aunt Anne Prescott; to Michael Glenn, Sara Glenn, and Susan Jhirad for their superior son as well as their support; to my boys, Linus and Tobit, best of koalas and headchogs; to my four parents—Jim Haber, Lydia Lake, Bob Edwards, and Susan Larson— for pretty much everything; and especially to my sister, Deborah Haber, for her spot-on critiques, her friendship, and her continual and much appreciated encouragement.

This novel was largely written in two great coffee houses in Somerville, Massachusetts, Café Rustica and the Sherman Café, and transcribed on a computer purchased with a grant from the Somerville Arts Council. Thanks to you all.